Goddess Girls

MEDUSA THE RICH

Goddess Girls

MEDUSA
THE
RICH

JOAN HOLUB & SUZANNE WILLIAMS

Aladdin

NEW YORK   LONDON   TORONTO   SYDNEY   NEW DELHI

ALADDIN

An imprint of Simon & Schuster Children's Publishing Division

1230 Avenue of the Americas, New York, NY 10020

First Aladdin hardcover edition April 2015

Text copyright © 2015 by Joan Holub and Suzanne Williams

Jacket illustrations © 2015 by Glenn Hanson

Also available in an Aladdin paperback edition.

All rights reserved, including the right of reproduction in whole or in part in any form.

ALADDIN is a trademark of Simon & Schuster, Inc.,

and related logo is a registered trademark of Simon & Schuster, Inc.

For information about special discounts for bulk purchases, please contact

Simon & Schuster Special Sales at 1-866-506-1949 or business@simonandschuster.com.

The Simon & Schuster Speakers Bureau can bring authors to your live event.

For more information or to book an event, contact the Simon & Schuster Speakers Bureau

at 1-866-248-3049 or visit our website at www.simonspeakers.com.

Book design by Karin Paprocki

The text of this book was set in Baskerville.

Manufactured in the United States of America 0315 FFG

2 4 6 8 10 9 7 5 3 1

Library of Congress Control Number 2014953870

ISBN 978-1-4424-8830-4 (hc)

ISBN 978-1-4424-8829-8 (pbk)

ISBN 978-1-4424-8831-1 (eBook)

For our mega-terrific fans!

*Rachael C., Micci S., Kylie S., Caitlin R. & Hannah R.,
Erin P. & Savanna B., Caitlynn L., Danielle H., McKay O.
& Reese O., Lorelai M., Lily-Ann & Mommy S., Kaitlyn W.,
Chelsea W., Sanskriti J., Shelly B., Megan D., Chelsea G. & Ivy
H., Lillia L., Haley G., Riley G., Renee G., Alexa M., Madison
W., Kaylee S., Sabrina E. & Sophia E., Jenny C., Jasmine C.,
Erin K. & Kristen S., Michelle J., Ella S., Lea S., Grace H.,
Isla B., Lana W., Lida L., Raven G., Himeko O., Athena E.,
Niki K., Shelby J., Virginia J., Sophia O., Sophie G.,
Roxie C. & Mari C., Ariel C., Jolene A. & Juliana A., Eden
O., The Andrade Family & Alba C., Ryanna L. & April L.,
Alexandra S., Emily M., Daniel M. & Zoila M., Paris O.,
Evilynn R., Christine D-H. & Khanya S., Vivian Z., Diamond
C., Jasmine R., Andrea Z., Paola F., Winter P., Ally M.,
Sabrina C., Angela C., Keyra M., Meghan B., Medori W., Abby
G., Jessie F., Shiresa.M.C., T.A., Anh H., Lan Anh H.,
Janeya B., Lily T., and you!*

—J.H. and S.W.

CONTENTS

Goddess Girls

MEDUSA
THE
RICH

1
Queen of Mean

SNAP! SNAP! SNAP! **THE SNAKES ON TOP OF** twelve-year-old Medusa's head gobbled down the handful of dried peas she tossed up to them as she sat cross-legged on the floor of her dorm room at Mount Olympus Academy one Friday afternoon. Though her snakes had been the result of an accident with Snakeypoo, a botched invention of the brainy goddessgirl Athena's—it had turned out to be a *happy* accident. Medusa adored the dozen snakes that had replaced her hair. She'd even given them all names: Viper, Flicka, Pretzel, Snapper, Twister, Slinky, Lasso, Slither, Scaly, Emerald, Sweetpea, and Wiggle! They were her pets now, and she couldn't imagine life without them.

"Help me choose?" she asked them as she dug through a box of comic-scrolls she'd written and drawn over the years. (Some she'd created when she was just six years old!) "Don't be too nice. If you don't like something, say so, okay? Only my ten very best ones can go into the collection I'm submitting to the Comicontest."

Eager to help as always, her snakes wriggled their heads forward for a better look as she pulled out a comic-scroll and unrolled it.

"Ooh! Remember this one?" The comic was one of

her favorites, drawn after she'd given Zeus a winged horse named Pegasus on the day of his wedding. "It's the one where Principal Zeus granted my wish to become immortal as a thank-you for my wedding present." Zeus was not only the principal of MOA; he was also King of the Gods and Ruler of the Heavens, which meant he had the power to do such things. "I was immortal only for a single day. But still. Good times." She sighed happily.

Medusa shifted to lie on her stomach. The comic-scroll was titled The Queen of Mean (episode #25): *Immortal for a Day*. Starring her—as the Queen of Mean! In this episode the queen had gotten her chance to be a goddessgirl for one day, thanks to Zeus. Like almost all of her comics, this one was autobiographical—loosely based on things that had happened to Medusa in real life. The queen looked like her and was a superhero who used something called payback magic to get even with dastardly evildoers. A magic cheese was one of her coolest—and stinkiest—weapons.

As her snakes followed along, Medusa began to read the best parts of the comic aloud to them in a dramatic voice:

"'Discovering that she can suddenly make winged sandals fly without help (something she's never been able to do before Zeus made her immortal), the Queen of Mean laces them on. She buzzes around the Mount Olympus Academy courtyard, doing awesome flips and tricks in midair that no one at MOA has ever seen before! *Voom! Boinggg! Zonk!*'" Medusa made fun sound effects to indicate the tricky flips. "'Then the queen zooms home to Greece.'"

Now Medusa switched to speak in a higher-toned

voice, the one she imagined the queen would use:

"'I vow to use my amazing powers to fight evil,'" says the Queen of Mean. "And also vow to show them off sometimes!'"

Medusa went on, switching back and forth between a normal narrator voice and the queen's voice. All the while her snakes gazed intently at her drawings.

"'When the queen gets to Greece, a seal herder named Proteus is terrorizing her poor parents. *No problem!* thinks the queen. She whips out her magic cheese and shouts the magic word—"Gorgonzola!" *Poof!* "Take that, Proteus. How does it feel to be vaporized?"'"

"Of course, Proteus doesn't reply because he's vapor now, and vapor can't talk," Medusa reminded her snakes before continuing with her comic. "Afterward my mom—that is, the *queen's* mom—says,

'Thank you for saving us, Queen of Mean. You rock!'
Then her dad grunts as usual, but in a happy way
this time. Next the queen's parents take down the
pictures of their other two immortal daughters,
Spinno and Ukelele, and toss them into the trash.
And they hang a humongous picture of the queen on
their wall instead."

Medusa paused, feeling a little pang of disappointment. Why couldn't it really be that way? But
no, in real life her parents' tossing out her sisters' pictures and hanging a big one of her was probably the
least likely thing in the comic to ever really happen.
Her parents had always favored her two sisters—who
were actually named Stheno and Euryale—over her.
Probably because her sisters were immortal and she
wasn't. In her comic-scrolls she could remake the
world however she wanted. Which meant she could

be an immortal superhero with parents who adored her!

Glancing up, she saw how fascinated her snakes were with her story, so she continued:

"'When the queen returns to Mount Olympus Academy that night, exhausted from her crime fighting, the four most popular goddessgirls at MOA—Athena, Persephone, Aphrodite, and Artemis—run over to her.

"Oh, please, please hang out with us at the Supernatural Market, or we'll just die!" they beg.' Immortals can't actually die," Medusa reminded her snakes. "But still. 'The queen goes with the four goddessgirls just to cut them a break. And that cute godboy Dionysus just happens to be there. And he just happens to save her a seat by him, which happens to be mega-cool with her. Later the queen visits

Hephaestus to do one last thing before her epic day of being immortal is over.'"

Medusa switched back to the superhero voice of her star character again: ""Hephaestus? Since you're the godboy of blacksmithing, how about forging a sparkly charm for me? Not one of those GG charms like Athena and her friends wear. Instead make mine an awesome one-of-a-kind charm. One with the letters *QoM*.' So he does. THE END.'"

SNAP! Medusa let go of the comic-scroll, and it rolled itself back up.

Smiling to herself, she pushed up to sit cross-legged again and then pulled up on the delicate gold chain around her throat. She ran her fingers over the sparkly gold, swirly letters of the QoM charm dangling from it. Though not everything she'd imagined herself doing on her day as an immortal had actually happened in real life, Hephaestus really *had* made this charm for her. And she'd flown in winged sandals all by herself too. And that cute boy Dionysus had become her crush!

People often asked her what the QoM charm stood for, but she'd never told anyone, not even Dionysus. It was her secret. Ha-ha-ha! Though that secret would soon be out if, by some huge miracle, she really did win the Comicontest.

It was sponsored by a group called Big D Publications. The prize was a publishing contract! Which she figured meant that Big D would make many copies of the winning comic collection to sell as scrollbooks in stores. The scrollbooks would probably end up in libraries everywhere too!

Then everyone would know about the Queen of Mean. Would they guess Medusa was really writing about herself? Probably. But who cared! Winning meant she'd be famous. And hopefully rich!

"So what do you think?" she asked her snakes.

Curling forward so she could see them better, they bunched themselves into a giant fist with only Slinky sticking straight up—their version of a thumbs-up.

She grinned. "Thanks, guys." Of course, they liked *every* comic she drew, especially the ones they starred in. And there were many of those. She frowned at her comic-scroll drawings. They were better—certainly more detailed—than the mostly stick figures with big O-shaped heads that she'd drawn at age six. But were they good enough to win the contest?

Others she'd selected included a comic where the Queen of Mean rescued a scaredy-cat boy named Poor Seidon (a thinly veiled reference to her ex-crush, the drippy godboy Poseidon) from a sea serpent threatening to toss him onto some jagged rocks. And in another one she and her faithful snakes foiled two evil candy-store-robbing sisters. (Modeled on guess who? Hint: Their names began with *S* and *E*!)

After setting her *Immortal for a Day* scroll in the "contest-worthy" pile, she counted how many good scrolls she'd chosen so far. "That makes nine. Still one comic-scroll short." She sighed. "Ten *good* comic-scrolls is a lot to come up with."

She'd been through everything, and her reject pile was huge. "Guess I'll have to make a new one," she mused aloud. "Needs to be something with adventure, drama, and a dash of humor, too. But what?"

Hmm. She tapped her chin with a fingertip, thinking. She didn't have much time. Entries had to be put in the contest box that sat in the center atrium at the Immortal Marketplace by tomorrow! There was another problem too. As usual she was practically broke. No way could she cover the fifteen-drachma entry fee. She let out a huff.

Sensing her frustration, Flicka, Pretzel, and Sweetpea dropped down to gently wind themselves around her neck like a collar. Slither, Emerald, and Wiggle nuzzled her cheeks. Her other six snakes patted the top of her head soothingly.

"Thanks, guys. You always know how to make me feel better," Medusa told them, smiling a little.

Huh? She jumped in surprise when a sharp knock came at her door.

"You in there, Snakehead?" her sister Stheno called. "You've got a little job to do for Euryale and me, remember? And you're late!"

Ye gods! Medusa had forgotten all about that.

Probably because this particular job wasn't something she'd wanted to remember.

"Coming!" she called back. Leaving her scrolls in the middle of the floor, she reluctantly got to her feet and left her room. If only she could win that contest. It would prove to everyone at MOA that although she didn't have immortal gifts, she did possess *some* creative talent. And then maybe even her sisters would treat her with more respect.

All she needed was some inspiration for a phantasmagoric, awesomerrific, super-dupertastic idea for that tenth comic. And she needed it fast!

2
A Care Package

MAKE SURE YOU GET ALL THE DUST BUNNIES under my bed. You missed some last time," Medusa's sister Euryale told her. Propped against two green satin-covered pillows, Euryale was lounging on her bed, lazily turning the pages of an old *Teen Scrollazine* while keeping one eye on Medusa as she cleaned.

It wasn't exactly the way Medusa wanted to spend the next hour. But to pay off a debt she owed to her sisters, she'd reluctantly agreed to clean their room fifteen times. This was the thirteenth time. Only two more to go after this one.

Medusa poked her broom beneath Euryale's bed and swept it back and forth. In addition to dust bunnies, she found several wadded-up homework papers, a barely used tube of green lip gloss, lots of ambrosia chip crumbs, and a half-eaten carrot. Holding up the carrot, she joked, "So I guess this must be what you feed your dust bunnies to make them get so big?"

Euryale scowled at her. "Ha-ha. You are so not hilarious."

Spying the lip gloss, Stheno, who'd been filing her nails, slid off her bed on the other side of the room and scooped it up. "Hey, I wondered where that got to!" She glowered at Euryale as if she suspected her sister of thievery.

15

But Medusa figured it was more likely that Stheno had just dropped the lip gloss onto the floor herself some time ago and hadn't noticed when it had rolled under Euryale's bed. Her sisters were careless with their belongings. Probably because, unlike her, they had so many of them.

Euryale and Stheno looked a lot like Medusa, which made sense since they were triplets. They all had the same light green skin and green eyes, and they had similar facial features. But whereas Medusa had snakes for hair, her sisters' hair was non-wiggly and didn't hiss. And, of course, they were immortal, while she was a mere mortal. So they could perform all kinds of magic that she couldn't do. A fact they enjoyed reminding her of as often as possible.

After Stheno pocketed her lip gloss, she hopped back onto her bed to continue filing her nails. But then she paused to point one end of her nail file toward a gloppy mess on top of her desk. "Don't forget to wipe up that spill," she told Medusa.

"Eew!" Medusa groaned. It looked like Stheno had spilled half a carton of ambrosia dip on her desk. And instead of cleaning it up right away, she'd just left it there for Medusa to deal with!

"Oh, quit complaining," said Stheno.

"Yeah," said Euryale.

Medusa didn't really have any choice but to obey. However, when her sisters weren't looking, she defiantly kicked Euryale's wadded-up homework papers back under her bed.

The reason she owed them so many room-cleanings was because they'd cast some spells a while back on her behalf. Spells that had caused some blabby gift box puppets and some guards at the Immortal Marketplace to forget that her snakes had tried to shoplift an expensive gold thunderbolt holder. She'd wanted to give it to Zeus as a wedding present—one she could never have afforded to buy him in a zillion years. When she'd caught her snakes dragging the holder behind her, she'd left it where it belonged—in the gift store. Anyway, they hadn't known that what they were doing was wrong. They'd only been trying to help her give Zeus a worthy gift!

As she wiped up the mess on Stheno's desk now, Medusa accidentally-on-purpose let a little of the gooey ambrosia dip drip onto a sandal her sister had left on the floor below her desk. With any luck Stheno would stick her foot in it. Ha! That would serve her right.

Just then a knock sounded at the door. "A big box came for you!" a girl's voice called out. A second girl's voice added, "By Hermes' Delivery Service chariot!"

There was a *thump* as the two girls set the box next to the door. Then their footsteps died away down the hall. Hermes had obviously gotten a couple of girls who lived here on the fourth floor to bring the box, since guys weren't allowed in the girls' hall.

Stheno leaped from her bed and flung open the door to eye the box in delight. "Yay! It's our weekly care package from Mom and Dad!" she sang out.

"Oh, goody," Medusa said unenthusiastically, because when Stheno had said "our," she'd only meant her and Euryale. *Not* Medusa. *Her* name was never included in the address on these weekly packages. In all her years at the Academy, her parents hadn't once sent her a package, letter, or card. Not even for her birthday, which she shared with her two sisters.

Stheno and Euryale dragged the box into the

room, ripped it open, and started pulling out all kinds of goodies. As Medusa looked on, they gleefully dug out sweets like Nectarpops and Ambrosia Chews, bags of Ambritos brand snack chips, and bottles of a supersweet, syrupy drink they all loved called NectarFizz. There were also new school supplies, clothing, and issues of the latest *Teen Scrollazine*.

"There's a letterscroll, too," Euryale announced. She pulled it from the bottom of the box once they'd emptied it and all their spoils lay scattered about the room.

"Read it out loud," Stheno said as she tried on a flowery green chiton that had been in the box.

"Okay," said Euryale.

Medusa cocked an ear to listen. Meanwhile she flicked a cloth here and there, pretending to dust her sisters' bookshelves. But really, she was just spreading the dust around.

When Euryale unrolled the letterscroll, a shower of coins that had been rolled up inside it dropped to the floor. As Euryale gathered the coins and tucked them into her pocket for safekeeping, Medusa eyed them, feeling even greener than usual—with envy!

Finally her sister got around to reading the letter aloud:

"DEAR STHENO AND EURYALE,

WE HOPE THIS CARE PACKAGE FINDS YOU WELL. WE ARE SO PROUD OF ALL YOUR HARD WORK AT SCHOOL AND YOUR EXCELLENT MARKS. WE'VE ENCLOSED YOUR USUAL ALLOWANCE IN CASE YOU NEED TO BUY ANYTHING WE'VE FORGOTTEN TO INCLUDE. LOOKING FORWARD TO SEEING YOU ON YOUR

NEXT VISIT HOME.

LOVE YOU TO PIECES!

MOM AND DAD

P.S. ALMOST FORGOT. PLEASE SEE THAT

DUSA GETS HER USUAL THREE OBELOI."

"Dusa" was their parents' nickname for Medusa. And the three obeloi they'd sent for her was a mere pittance, only half a drachma. It was just one third of the allowance each of her sisters got. Added to the few obols she'd managed to save from her previous weekly allowances, it still wasn't anywhere near enough to pay the Comicontest entry fee. Same old story. While her sisters practically wallowed in money, she never had enough.

After flinging the letterscroll onto her bed, Euryale reached in her pocket. "Here you go," she said, handing Medusa three small silver coins.

"Oh, joy," Medusa muttered under her breath as she stuck her allowance in her pocket.

Across the room her sister counted out the remaining coins, splitting them with Stheno. "Nine for you; nine for me," she said, handing her sister a share of the loot.

Then Euryale snuggled back against the pillows on her bed with a bag of Ambritos. After tearing it open, she munched on a handful of the chips. "Want some, Dusa?" she mumbled with her mouth full when she saw Medusa staring.

"Sure," Medusa said eagerly. Euryale held the bag out to her. However, when Medusa reached for it, Euryale snatched it away, laughing. Her sisters got a kick out of teasing her like that.

"Ha-ha. Thanks for nothing," Medusa said coldly.

Then, to cover up for the hurt of being left out of her parents' affections, she added, "You can keep all the stuff in your stupid I-don't-care package. I don't need it!" Privately she considered sneaking a few of the treats when her sisters' backs were turned, but that would be thieving, and she was no thief. Besides, her snakes would see, and she was trying to set a good example for them. No way did she want them to attempt shoplifting ever again!

"You're just jealous," Stheno said. After carelessly tossing her brand-new flowery green chiton over the back of her desk chair, she flopped down onto her bed opposite Euryale's and opened one of the new *Teen Scrollazine*s their parents had sent.

"Am not," Medusa grumbled. But she knew it was a lie. Though she tried not to dwell on the injustice of how much her parents favored her sisters, she couldn't help thinking how nice it would be to have parents who doted on *her*, showering her with the kind of stuff her sisters always got. But that was never going to happen. When both of her sisters' heads were turned, she balled up her dirty dusting cloth and stuck it into the pocket of Stheno's new chiton.

She jumped when Stheno looked over suddenly and asked, "What are you doing with my new chiton?"

"Just going to hang it up," Medusa replied innocently. She took the chiton to the closet to do just that, but then let it slip off its hanger to the closet floor when her sisters looked away.

Euryale picked up a new *Teen Scrollazine* and started to leaf through it. It was a duplicate of the one Stheno was reading. Their parents always included two copies of each new issue so that her two sisters wouldn't have to share. Must be nice!

Face it, she told herself sternly. She was stuck with the family she had, and none of them was ever going to change. And really, she should be used to it by now. Back home her room was a closet (literally!). By contrast, her sisters had grown up sharing a cute room with twin beds covered with frilly green bedspreads, and shelves of books, toys, and dolls.

Being a mortal, Medusa just didn't count in her family. But someday, when she was all grown up and a famous comic-scroll author, she would buy herself her very own care package filled with all her favorite things.

3

Silenus

JUST AS MEDUSA WAS ABOUT TO DECLARE THAT she had finished cleaning, Stheno popped the top off a bottle of NectarFizz. "Oops!" she called out as the syrupy drink sprayed all over the rug between her and Euryale's beds. "Wipe that up, will you, Dusa?" She turned another page of her scrollazine.

Medusa let out a displeased huff. But she grabbed the cleaning sponge and went down on her knees.

As she was scrubbing at the spill, there was another knock at the door.

"Enter!" Stheno called out.

At the exact same moment the door opened, Euryale said to Medusa, "Don't forget to empty our trash can when you're done with that."

Glancing up, Medusa saw Artemis standing awkwardly in the doorway. Her archery bow and quiver of arrows were slung over her shoulders as usual. And her glossy black hair was encircled by golden bands that caught it up in its customary cute twist at the back of her head.

"Oh, there you are," she said to Medusa after a moment's pause. Though she acted as if nothing were amiss, it was obvious she had taken in the scene and overheard what Euryale had said.

Medusa's cheeks flushed. She dropped her

sponge and jumped to her feet. *Godsamighty!* She must have looked like she was her sisters' servant! Which she kind of was, but only temporarily. Before she could think what to say to cover her embarrass-ment, Artemis nodded toward the far end of the hallway.

"Dionysus is looking for you," she said. "I ran into him outside the dorm when I was coming upstairs just now. Told him I'd check your room. Only, you weren't there, so I—"

"I'll go see what he wants," interrupted Medusa. She tossed the sponge in a high arc to land on Euryale's desk. In two steps she was at the door, where Artemis still waited.

"Hey!" Euryale protested.

"But you haven't finishing clean—" Stheno started to say.

Medusa cut them off. "Don't be pathetic," she called to them over her shoulder. "I only volunteered to help you out this once." She spoke in a voice loud enough for Artemis and anyone else who might be lurking in the hall to hear. "Watch and learn, I said. Good housekeeping is a valuable skill. With more practice even you two mess-monsters might someday master it." Quickly she swept out of the room before her sisters could retaliate. She knew they'd make her pay for what she'd said, but seeing their shocked faces just now had been worth it.

"Is everything okay?" Artemis asked hesitantly once Medusa shut her sisters' door firmly behind her. "Between you and your sisters, I mean?"

"Sure. Why wouldn't it be?" Medusa snapped as they both headed up the hall. She was still embarrassed about what Artemis had seen and heard.

"No reason," Artemis said, backing off a little. But then she added, "I'm glad Apollo doesn't treat me like your sisters treat you sometimes. They're something else!"

"You can say that again," Medusa agreed ruefully. She gave Artemis a small smile, glad for the acknowledgment of how difficult her sisters could be. Artemis's brother, Apollo, was way nicer than Stheno or Euryale, or so it seemed to Medusa. Still, she didn't tell Artemis *why* she had been cleaning her sisters' room. Besides not wanting this goddessgirl's pity, Medusa didn't want to sound whiny.

"Later, then," Artemis said when they'd reached her room.

"Thanks for coming to find me . . . ," Medusa began, but her words were drowned out by sudden barking.

As soon as Artemis had opened the door to her room, her three dogs had leaped around her in the hall, licking her hands and wagging their tails. They seemed overjoyed to see her, even though she probably hadn't left them for long. Medusa smiled to herself, thinking how glad she was that she and her snakes *never* had to be parted from one another.

At the end of the hall, she pushed through the door to the stairway and found Dionysus sitting on the landing beyond. He sprang to his feet when the door opened. "Oh, good. Artemis found you," he said, his violet eyes shining with excitement.

Medusa's heart skipped a beat like it always did when she hadn't seen this brown-haired, violet-eyed godboy in a while. In this case "a while" meant since lunch. She still found it hard to believe that such a cute, popular, and fun-loving godboy was in like with *her*. "What's up?" she asked.

"Good news!" he told her excitedly. "Silenus has been found!"

"Your pet goat?" Medusa asked him. "The missing one?"

Dionysus had told her about the pet goat he'd gotten when he was a four-year-old child being raised by nymphs in a hidden valley on Earth. He and Silenus had been inseparable from the start, wandering everywhere together. And once, when they'd become lost in a sudden snowstorm high on a mountain, Silenus had saved Dionysus's life by keeping him warm until the storm had passed and they could find their way back to the valley again. So it was no surprise that Dionysus had been heartbroken when, during a weekend visit home recently, the nymphs had informed him that his goat had disappeared.

"Yeah. That's what my news is about. He's not missing anymore! Dionysus said in reply to her question.

"Oh! I'm so glad," she said. "I can't imagine what it would be like to lose my snakes. Luckily there's no chance of that, since they're firmly attached to my head."

Dionysus laughed. "Come get a snack in the cafeteria with me, okay? I'll tell you what happened."

"Okay," said Medusa. She didn't want to stick around the dorm anyway, just in case her sisters decided to come after her. They were probably too lazy to bother, though. She'd bet anything they were still on their beds, reading their new scrollazines and eating snacks. Or maybe they were planning a way to get even with her for what she'd just done. Whatever!

Giving her the dimpled smile that Medusa adored, Dionysus took her hand, and they started downstairs together. "So this king in Phrygia named Midas sent me a letterscroll a few minutes ago," he said as they walked. "He found Silenus wandering around in his rose garden yesterday. Can you believe it? I have no idea how he got there. But I'm going to go get him."

"Now?" she asked. When he nodded, she couldn't help feeling a stab of disappointment. She was glad her crush was going to get his pet back. Still, since it was Friday, she'd hoped they'd go to the Supernatural Market for shakes later with their friends. But Phrygia was across the Aegean Sea in Asia Minor. Not a quick trip. He wouldn't make it back in time to hang out.

As they reached the main floor and headed down the hall to the cafeteria, she got an idea. "Think you'll need help?" she asked.

He raised an eyebrow. "Are you offering to come?"

he said as they pushed into the empty cafeteria.

She smiled at the hopeful note in his voice. "Don't sound so surprised," she said. "Of course I will." Then she added, "If you want me to." She scanned the snacks table. There was a huge bowl of fruit, mini hero sandwiches, and a large platter of freshly baked ambrosia turnovers. She grabbed a tart, green apple and crunched into it.

Mmm. The more sour, the better, as far as she was concerned. She knew some people might say that her taste in apples mirrored her personality. Not so! Though she seldom sugar-coated her opinions about things, that did *not* make her sour.

"Are you kidding?" said Dionysus. "That would be mega-awesome! And I'm sure Zeus won't mind either." He took a bite of his turnover. "Ye gods. These are great!"

"Oh yeah. Zeus. I almost forgot I'd need his permission to go on such a long trip. You will too, right?" She took another bite of her apple.

"Done. I was going to go by winged sandal," Dionysus said, "but when I told Zeus about the trip a few minutes ago, he volunteered to take me in one of the school chariots. Turns out he's heading to a temple ceremony in Aizanoi, which isn't far from Phrygia. He'll drop me at King Midas's palace before he flies on to the temple, then pick me up to return to MOA tomorrow morning."

"So this'll be an overnight trip?" Medusa asked. "I'll need to pack a few things, then . . . if you really think Principal Zeus will let me—"

"LET YOU DO WHAT?" boomed a voice as loud as thunder. Startled, Medusa and Dionysus turned sharply to see Zeus burst through the cafeteria doors and come toward them. Seven feet tall, with bulging muscles, wild red hair, and a piercing gaze, he was always an intimidating sight.

"Ready to go?" he asked Dionysus.

"Just need to run upstairs and grab my bag," Dionysus told him.

"Good," said Zeus. He turned his blazing blue eyes on Medusa. "Well?" he asked her. "You look like you have something on your mind. Speak!"

"I . . . uh . . ." Thrown off guard by his abrupt manner (as well as his formidable appearance), Medusa just stood there, rooted to the spot and unable to answer. Even her snakes went still. It was as though she'd turned her stony gaze—which could turn mortals to stone in an instant if she weren't wearing her protective stoneglasses—on herself!

Seeing that she was at a loss for words, Dionysus

came to her rescue. "Medusa and I were kind of wondering if she could come with me."

To her surprise Zeus replied, "I don't see why not." His eyes lit up at the sight of the snacks table, and he grabbed a couple of turnovers. After stuffing one into his mouth, he mumbled, "Mee me owside. Coryar. Twenny mints." Then he turned on his heel and marched back out the cafeteria doors.

"Meet him outside in the courtyard in twenty minutes," Dionysus translated in case she hadn't understood. "We'd better get a move on!"

"Thanks for the save," Medusa said as they hurried out of the cafeteria and up the stairs again. "My brain froze."

"No problemo, greenie-girl," Dionysus replied gallantly.

She smiled. She loved it when he called her that!

"See you in the courtyard," he said once they'd reached the fourth-floor landing. There he split off and took the stairs two at a time up to the boys' fifth-floor dorm.

Medusa dashed down the hall, slowing only to tip-toe past her sisters' room. Luckily, their door was still closed tight. *Phew!* She made it to her room without incident. She grabbed her overnight bag, opened it on her bed, and tossed in some clothes, plus snacks for her snakes, and a toothbrush.

Then she plucked her green wool cloak from a peg on the back of her door in case it got windy and cold during the journey. Folding it over one arm, she turned back to her bed to pick up her bag.

Her eyes fell on the comic-scrolls still sitting in the middle of the floor. She'd gotten so caught up in Dionysus's story that she'd forgotten she still had a story to write of her own. One for the contest. *Hmm.* Maybe she shouldn't go with him after all.

But then she had a thought. If she was lucky and kept her eyes peeled, maybe the trip to Phrygia would give her an idea for that tenth comic-scroll she needed to complete her contest entry. If so, she could work on it while staying at King Midas's palace! She snatched up a blank scroll and tossed it into her bag too.

After locking her door behind her, Medusa headed down the hall again. Unfortunately, this time when she neared her sisters' room, Stheno flung open their door as if she'd been lying in wait.

Her eyes fell on Medusa's overnight bag and cloak. "Hey! Where do you think you're going?"

Euryale poked her head out and added, "Yeah. There's still a mess in here you need to clean up or it doesn't count as an official cleaning."

"Oh, sorry. But I'm off to Phrygia," Medusa informed them with fake sweetness. "Zeus invited me," she added, though that wasn't exactly true. "He's got a temple ceremony near there to attend. And he's waiting for me and Dionysus right now. But if you want me to tell him I can't go because you think your room is more important . . ." She hadn't *said* she and Dionysus were actually invited to the temple ceremony itself, but she'd implied it.

"You're lying," Euryale accused.

"Just look out your window if you don't believe me," Medusa challenged. "He'll be out in the court-yard getting ready to leave."

As Euryale went to check, Stheno stayed in the hall, eyeing Medusa to make sure she didn't sneak off. "What do you see?" Stheno called to Euryale after a minute.

"She's right," Euryale called back reluctantly. "Zeus is out there and he's hooking Pegasus up to one of the school chariots."

"Humph." Stheno flipped her long green hair back and stared hard at Medusa. "I don't know why Zeus would invite *you* to go to a temple ceremony," she said peevishly.

Medusa shrugged and slipped by her, then called over her shoulder. "What can I say? Maybe he just likes me. I did give him an awesome wedding gift, you have to admit. You know how much he dotes on Pegasus."

"You better at least cover your head!" Stheno called after her in a parting shot.

Euryale snickered, having just returned to the hallway as Medusa reached the stair door. "Yeah, those slimy reptiles of yours might spook Pegasus!"

"Ha-ha," said Medusa, gritting her teeth. "And how many times do I have to tell you, they're *not* slimy."

Ssss! As if to emphasize her displeasure, her snakes hissed at her sisters, and flicked their tongues as well.

Medusa smiled to herself as she swung through the door and started down the marble staircase. It was plain that for once her sisters were jealous of her, instead of the other way around. *Sweet!*

4

Up and Away!

DIONYSUS SMILED, SHOWING HIS CUTE DIMPLES again, as Medusa came up to him and Zeus in the courtyard. She could tell her crush was superhappy about finding his pet goat, and she was happy for him too.

"Looks like we're almost ready," Dionysus announced. He took her bag from her and swung it up into the small deep-purple, single-benched chariot the two of them would be riding in. The MOA logo and a large gold thunderbolt were emblazoned on its side. Already hitched to the chariot, Pegasus pawed at the ground and fluttered his mighty golden wings as Zeus made some final adjustments to the harness.

Medusa went over to give the white horse a pat, and he gave a whinny of recognition. "Do you remember me, boy?" she asked. It was hard to believe that he'd once been a charm on a necklace she'd bought from seeing an ad in a *Teen Scrollazine*. The necklace was called the Immortalizer, and it was supposed to turn whoever wore it into an immortal. It hadn't worked on her, obviously, but it *had* brought the enchanted Pegasus to life.

"Course he does," Zeus said, giving his favorite horse a fond pat on the neck. "This guy never forgets a thing."

Pegasus pushed his big head toward Medusa and nuzzled her hand with his nose. Contrary to what her sisters had suggested, he didn't seem at all put off by her snaky hair. And her snakes weren't wary of him, either. In fact, Lasso, Sweetpea, and Slinky reached over and stroked his muzzle, while Snapper and Scaly stretched themselves out and gently head-bumped him in a fond greeting.

When Principal Zeus swung himself onto Pegasus's back, Medusa scurried to take her place beside Dionysus on the bench seat in the chariot. She'd barely sat down when the horse began to flap its mighty golden wings. Liftoff!

As their chariot soared into the air, she caught a glimpse of her sisters standing together at their dorm room window to watch the leave-taking. Leaning over, Medusa sent them a big wave and theatrically blew them a kiss. They drew back from the window in a hurry. She could just imagine how annoyed they were at seeing her take off like this in the company of the illustrious Principal Zeus!

"My sisters," Medusa explained as Dionysus gave her a curious look.

"Ah," he said. "It's cool that you guys are getting along better these days." She sent him an *Are you kidding?* look, but he'd switched his gaze toward the clear blue sky and didn't see.

Medusa's snakes wriggled happily as the chariot soared over the majestic five-story Academy. Built of polished white stone and surrounded on all sides by rows of Ionic columns, it was an awesome sight. Beyond it she saw a couple of dozen students— mostly boys—out on the sports fields. Some were scrambling up the ropes of a climbing net, some were lifting weights, and others were chucking spears as far as they could throw them. She nudged Dionysus and motioned toward them.

"Are they practicing for the Temple Games?" she asked. The upcoming series of athletic and adventure game competitions was still a couple of weeks away, but practice for them had already begun. Though the competitions were open to boys and girls alike, she didn't know of very many girls who had signed up to participate. A rainbow goddessgirl named Iris had. Artemis, too. She was down there now, drawing back her bowstring.

Dionysus was among the boys who had signed up. When he glanced down at the field, he said, "Yeah. Unfortunately, I'll have to miss this weekend's practices because of our trip." After a pause he shot her a quick look. "Um, did you hear that each contestant is allowed to pick someone to champion them at the games?"

Medusa shrugged, still watching Artemis. "Champion them how?" *Zing!* Artemis's arrow flew from her bow to hit the center of her target.

Woo-hoo! Medusa punched a fist into the air, whooping for her even though the goddessgirl couldn't hear her. Artemis was a superb archer, just like her twin brother, Apollo.

"I'm not really sure," Dionysus replied. "By cheering and stuff, I guess. Waving encouraging signs."

Medusa rolled her eyes. "Sounds dumb." As soon as the words were out of her mouth, she regretted them. She'd only been half-listening, really. But now Dionysus looked kind of taken aback. Like he was sorry he'd even brought it up.

His face was unreadable as he said, "Yeah, I

suppose it is." He reached into the pocket of his tunic and pulled out a rumpled letterscroll tied with a purple ribbon.

What if he'd been planning on asking *her* to be his champion? wondered Medusa as he unrolled the scroll. She actually wouldn't mind that. In fact, it might be kind of fun! She tried to backtrack. "Uh, did you mean . . . Were you going to ask—"

"I once asked Hera to be my champion at a chariot race," Zeus called back to them, apparently having overheard some of what they'd said. "She honored me greatly when she agreed. Not only did she gift me with the favor of her lace handkerchief to tie onto my chariot, but she also cheered more loudly for me than anyone else did during the race. Really got my spirits up." Their chariot entered some clouds just then, and he fell silent as he navigated their way out.

Still holding up his letterscroll, Dionysus turned a little in his seat to face Medusa. "This is the message King Midas sent me." He began reading aloud:

"DEAR DIONYSUS,

I FOUND A SCRUFFY-LOOKING WHITE

GOAT IN MY ROSE GARDEN THIS MORNING.

THERE WAS A TAG ON THE COLLAR

AROUND ITS NECK THAT READS: 'MY

NAME IS SILENUS. IF FOUND, PLEASE

CONTACT DIONYSUS AT MOUNT

OLYMPUS ACADEMY.'

YOU MAY COME TO GET SILENUS AT

YOUR EARLIEST CONVENIENCE. I WILL

TAKE GOOD CARE OF HIM UNTIL YOU

ARRIVE. I HAVE ENCLOSED A MAP WITH

DIRECTIONS TO MY PALACE.

Yours truly,

King Midas of Phrygia"

Principal Zeus must have overheard yet again, because he called over his shoulder, "Hey, could you pass that map up here? I think we might be slightly off course."

The scrap of papyrus on which the king had drawn his map had been wrapped inside the letter-scroll, so Dionysus removed it and passed it forward to Zeus. Then he glanced over at Medusa, saying, "Silenus was missing for so long, I'd almost given up hope of ever seeing him again. I—"

"What's this?" Zeus boomed, drawing their attention again. He was looking downward now, and he sounded very annoyed.

Because Pegasus was amazingly fast—much faster

than winged sandals or chariots pulled by other animals—they were already halfway over the sparkling blue waters of the Aegean Sea. Following Zeus's gaze, Medusa and Dionysus spotted a long wooden ship circling an island in the Aegean. An island on which a fine temple of white marble had been built.

The chariot swayed abruptly as Principal Zeus directed Pegasus to swoop low over the ship. It was flying a black-and-white skull-and-crossbones flag!

"Thought so," Zeus growled. "Pirates! I've received reports that they've been stealing riches from my temples lately, the dastardly devils. Well, not today!"

He reached into the thunderbolt holder strapped over his back and drew out a bolt. Taking aim, he hurled it at the ship with a mighty throw. *Ka-BOOM!*

As the thunderbolt struck the deck of the ship, flames sprang up. The pirates began running around.

The cowardly ones jumped overboard and swam away. But the braver ones rushed over with buckets of water to put out the fire.

"Score!" Dionysus cheered, punching a fist into the air as he watched the scene below.

"That'll keep you out of trouble for a while!" Zeus roared down at the pirates. He was grinning with glee as he took Pegasus higher again. Soon they'd crossed the Aegean and were flying inland over Asia Minor. Zeus consulted the map on the scrap of papyrus and guided the winged horse toward the location of the palace.

"Hey! I think I see the rose garden!" Medusa shouted a few minutes later. She pointed to a huge, gorgeous garden below them with rows and rows of rosebushes. Wow! There were hundreds of them, she realized.

"I see a cottage. But where's the king's palace?" Dionysus asked in confusion as Pegasus swooped in for a landing.

"Good question," said Zeus. No sooner had they touched down than the plain wooden door of the small thatch-roofed stone cottage opened. A tall, thin man with wavy brown hair and a beard appeared in the doorway. He was wearing a modest gold crown, which slipped sideways on his head as he and the small white goat that frolicked beside him came running to greet the visitors.

"Silenus! Buddy!" cried Dionysus. As soon as the goat heard his voice, it bounded over to him and butted its head against Dionysus in pleased recognition. *Maaa! Maaa!* it bleated happily. Dionysus bent and gave the goat a hug.

While they were having this joyous reunion, King

Midas greeted his other two guests warmly. He was obviously flustered when he recognized Zeus. "Welcome, welcome, your prominent eminence . . . er . . . your gracious and powerful mightiness . . . um . . . your most magnanimous and magnificent majesty of the heavens." As he spoke, he bowed up and down and up and down.

Zeus beamed, obviously pleased with King Midas's show of respect. "Thank you! You have done a great service to my student," Zeus said, gesturing a hand toward Dionysus and Silenus. They were now playing some kind of chasing game among the rosebushes. "If I could prevail on your hospitality," Zeus went on, "I would like to leave my two charges—Dionysus and Medusa—in your care for the night while I attend a ceremony in Aizanoi. I will return for them in the morning."

"Yes, yes, that would be fine!" exclaimed King Midas. He nodded so enthusiastically, bobbing his head up and down, up and down, that his crown slid this way and that. "I would be honored, oh most distinguished of all the divinities, most impressive and imperial of all immortals, most—"

"Excellent!" Zeus boomed, cutting him short. Abruptly he turned on his heel and strode toward Pegasus.

"Would you like some cake to take on your journey?" King Midas called after him. Then he added anxiously, "It wouldn't be nearly as fine as what you're used to, I imagine, but—"

Zeus paused, appearing to consider the idea. He had a major sweet tooth, Medusa knew. However, when the king informed him that the cake wasn't quite baked yet, he continued on. "Thanks, but no thanks. No time to lose." He unharnessed Pegasus and then, leaving the chariot behind for now, leaped onto the white horse's back. Then came a flap of mighty golden wings, and they were off again!

With a look of awe on his face, King Midas stared after them. Then his gaze returned to Medusa. Since he was mortal, she had taken her stoneglasses from her pocket and put them on just before they'd landed here. Turning one's host to stone would not have been very good manners, even if it happened by accident!

"Here, take these," said Midas, offering her a handful of freshly fallen rose petals he'd picked up. "I bet your snakes would enjoy a snack."

"Thanks," said Medusa. Taking the petals, she tossed them in the air and her snakes eagerly snapped them up. She was surprised and pleased that the king seemed unfazed by her snakes. Most mortals reacted to them with terror.

"Come, I'll take you and Dionysus inside my palace so I can show you to your rooms," Midas went on. "Then we can have an evening tea party in the garden with some of that cake. And with more snacks for your snakes."

Medusa's snakes wriggled in delight at the prospect of more rose petals. They obviously liked the king, and she'd always found them to be good judges of character. She smiled and nodded, accepting his invitation. Then he summoned Dionysus over, and Silenus tagged along. *Maaa! Maaa!*

Dionysus got his bag from the chariot and then reached for hers, but she picked it up before him. "That's okay. I can get it," she said.

As they followed King Midas inside the stone cottage "palace," she realized her crush had probably only been trying to be nice by helping her. She probably should have let him. That's what Aphrodite, the goddessgirl of love and beauty, would no doubt have done in her place. After all, crushes helped each other, and her bag *was* pretty heavy. *Drat.* Yet another mistake. She really stunk at this boy-girl stuff. Pretty soon Dionysus was going to think she didn't like him!

Dionysus's room was at the front of the cottage, Medusa's at the back. There was a central room between them that apparently served as a combination living room and dining room. It had three large overstuffed chairs set before a fireplace, and a linen-draped table with a sideboard. "But where will you sleep?" Medusa asked King Midas, noticing that there wasn't a third bedroom for him.

"Don't worry about me," he assured her. "I'll be

quite comfortable in my chair here before the fire. You go ahead and make yourselves at home. The kitchen's out back. I'm going to go have a word with my cook about that cake."

"But—" Medusa started to protest as the king went toward the rear door of the cottage.

Dionysus stopped her with a finger to his lips. "It would be an insult to him if we refused the accommodations he's offered," he whispered. "Just go with it."

She nodded, knowing he was right. After quickly unpacking her bag in her room, she rejoined Dionysus in the cottage's tiny living room area. "Do you think King Midas's kingdom is poor? Is that why his palace is a tiny cottage?"

"I've been wondering the same thing," Dionysus replied as they went to join the king.

Three places had been set with tea things on a

small white wicker table in the rose garden. Once everyone was seated, King Midas himself poured the tea. Soon his cook, a red-cheeked girl with long yellow hair, appeared bearing a big round cake. It was sunken in the middle, and when she cut it into slices and handed them around on plates, Medusa could see that the cake wasn't fully cooked.

However, King Midas only said, "Thank you, Tanis. This will do nicely."

After she left, he apologized, "Sorry about the cake. Tanis isn't really a gifted cook, but she needed a job."

Not really a gifted cook? Now, that was an understatement if she'd ever heard one, thought Medusa as she took a bite of the gooey half-raw cake. It was a good thing Zeus hadn't stayed to sample it. No way would he have been pleased.

"Her family's farm was especially hard hit during Typhon's recent rampages," King Midas went on. "As were many of the other farms and homes around here."

So that was it! Medusa realized. The reason the king was so poor.

Typhon was a monster of whirling tornado-strength winds who had escaped from imprisonment in the depths of the Underworld not long ago. He'd ravaged many lands before attacking MOA, too. Fortunately, with the help of Iris and her rainbows, as well as four seasonal wind brothers, Zeus had managed to capture the monster and imprison him once more—in a secret location. Hopefully, Typhon would never escape to make trouble again.

Medusa noticed that Dionysus was secretly feeding Silenus most of his cake under the table. Well, maybe *not* so secretly, since she'd seen what he was doing. At least someone liked the cake! Silenus was wolfing—er, goating it down!

"Typhon's winds also swept away my first palace—my *real* one," Midas continued. He sighed a little sadly. Then he smiled in Dionysus's direction. "But miraculously, my lovely rose gardens were spared. I would've been heartbroken had they been destroyed." Breaking off, he handed his plate with its barely touched cake to Dionysus. "Maybe Silenus would like some more?" he said with a wink.

After Silenus had enjoyed his second, and then his third slice of cake—courtesy of Medusa—King Midas showed her and Dionysus his favorite rosebushes.

"Inhale the roses' light, sweet scent," he invited.

Since snakes pick up smells partly through their tongues, Medusa's snakes practically wore their tongues out now. Flicking them through the air they strained to capture scents as heavenly as the taste of ambrosia and nectar.

"The goddessgirl Persephone back at MOA would *die* for a chance to see this garden," Medusa commented. Then she grinned, adding, "If she weren't immortal, that is." As the goddessgirl of spring and growing plants, gardens were Persephone's thing.

Dionysus grinned back. But before he could add anything, they heard a munching sound that made them all whirl around. "No, Silenus! Don't!" Dionysus scolded the goat. Despite having devoured three pieces of cake, the goat was now nibbling the rosebushes, too. He'd already left several plants lopsided or completely bare of roses.

A look of horror flitted across King Midas's face. But then he made the best of it and laughed. "Don't worry," he told Dionysus. "A bit of pruning never hurts roses. In fact, they'll grow back all the faster for it."

Before the goat could do any more damage, however, Medusa and Dionysus ran after him. Silenus took them on a merry chase through the bushes, eventually leading them back to the front door of the stone cottage, where the king waited. By then the sun was beginning to set and the air had grown cool.

"So when will your new palace be built?" Medusa asked the king, still breathless from the chase as they all entered the cottage.

"No time soon," King Midas said matter-of-factly. "It's much more important to rebuild the homes and farms of the villagers first. However, I *do* wish there were more money for that purpose." He sighed. "My royal treasury is running dangerously low after paying for the repairs and rebuilding already in progress. And that's just the beginning of what'll be needed."

So I'm not the only one with money problems, reflected Medusa. She had to admit, though, that King Midas's money problems sounded far worse than her own. The fee needed to enter a comic-scroll contest was nothing compared to the mounds of riches it would take to repair an entire kingdom!

The three of them had barely settled into the chairs around the fireplace, with Silenus curled up at Dionysus's feet, when a loud crash came from the direction of the garden. A girl's voice shouted, "Oh no! The teacups!"

"Excuse me," King Midas apologized as he rose from his chair. "I'd better go help Tanis clear the dishes."

"Sounds like she's about as gifted at clearing dishes

as she is at cooking," Medusa joked to Dionysus after Midas was out the door.

Dionysus laughed, which made Medusa smile. She loved to make him laugh. "Seriously, though," she added, "I wish there were something we could do for the king. Can't you use your godboy powers to help his kingdom somehow?"

"I've been thinking the same thing," Dionysus said as he reached down to pet Silenus. The goat's ears had perked up when he'd heard the crash, but he settled again. Probably too stuffed from all that he'd eaten to bother investigating curious sounds.

"And?" asked Medusa.

"And there *is* something I can do," said Dionysus. "To reward him for his hospitality and his kindness to Silenus, I was thinking I could grant him a wish."

"A magic wish? Awesome idea. I say do it," Medusa urged him.

"Do what?" the king asked as he stepped through the door carrying a tray full of broken crockery. He set the tray down on the table near the chairs as Dionysus explained.

"I must say, that's a very nice offer," the king said after Dionysus had finished. "But I've enjoyed taking care of Silenus, and I'm delighted to spend the evening with the two of you. Why should I receive a reward for being kind, when kindness is its own reward?"

"What? No! You have to take it! I mean, those are very fine thoughts," Medusa said. Then in her usual blunt manner she added, "but kindness alone won't rebuild your kingdom or help your people." She paused. "Money could, though."

"Oh!" said King Midas. His eyes went wide. "I see what you mean!" He furrowed his brow as if thinking. Finally he leaned forward in his chair and spoke to Dionysus. "I accept your offer. And I know exactly what to wish for."

"Speak it," Dionysus commanded.

"Well, everyone says I have the right touch when it comes to growing roses," Midas said slowly. "They say I have a green thumb." He paused. "So I was wondering . . . could I wish to have the right touch for growing gold, too? Could you grant me a *golden touch*? So that whatever I touch with my fingertip turns to gold?" He held up his right index finger.

Medusa's eyes lit up. "Ooh! Perfect. Can you do that, Dionysus?"

A little cloud of concern passed over the godboy's face, but it disappeared so quickly that she wondered if she'd only imagined it. "Yes, but are you sure?" Dionysus asked the king. "You'll only get a single wish, and once that wish goes into effect, there will be no take-backs."

"Why would he want to give up such a glorious power, once bestowed?" Medusa interrupted. "That would be crazy!"

King Midas seemed encouraged by her confidence in his idea. He nodded enthusiastically. "Yes! I'm sure it's what I want."

"All right, then." With a look of intense concentration on his face, Dionysus reached out, pointing the index finger of his right hand at the king. "Hold your hand out to mine," he instructed. When Midas did, Dionysus pulled back a little and added, "Last chance to change your mind."

"I won't. I'm sure," said Midas.

"He said he's sure," Medusa confirmed. She could hardly wait for the king to finally get a bit of luck. A fingertip's worth!

"Okay. Here goes." Dionysus touched the tip of his right index finger to the tip of King Midas's right index finger. There was a slight glow where their fingers met, just for a split second. Then Dionysus let his hand fall to his side again.

Midas faltered, looking unsure. Then he lowered his hand too.

"That's it?" he and Medusa asked at the same time.

Dionysus nodded and smiled at the king. "Your touch is now as good as gold."

With his hand outstretched in front of him, Midas ran to the dining room table and touched a piece of a broken teacup. He and Medusa stared eagerly at it for a long minute, hardly daring to breathe.

"Nothing's happening," she finally announced, disappointed.

Dionysus smiled. Sounding unworried, he told the king, "The magic takes a while to work. Overnight should do it. By the time you wake in the morning, I guarantee you'll have the golden touch."

"The golden touch," Medusa repeated dreamily. She liked the sound of that. It had a certain ring to it. A *golden* ring in fact.

5
The Golden Touch

AFTER A SIMPLE DINNER, THEY ALL WENT TO

their rooms for the night. But Medusa didn't go to bed

right away. Feeling a burst of inspiration, she got out

her blank scroll and pen. Because she had just gotten

an idea for that tenth comic she needed to enter the

Comicontest! Words and pictures flowed fast from her

pen as she pulled ideas from the events of the day and

mixed them with ideas from her imagination.

First she had the Queen of Mean use her magic Gorgonzola cheese to rescue a king (one who looked very much like King Midas in her drawings) from a gigantic, terrifying monster. A monster that looked like Typhon and broke dishes and ate everything else in its path. It even tried to eat a sweet little pet goat! But when the monster nibbled on the queen's magic cheese . . . the cheese exploded! The surprised look she drew on the monster's face was totally hilarious!

When she'd finished her new comic-scroll, Medusa looked it over carefully. *Perfect!* she thought. She finally had the last comic she needed. It had lots of action. Plenty of humor. Good pacing. It would make a great addition to her collection for the Comicontest, if she did say so herself.

Daylight was flooding her room through the

sheer curtains by the time she rose the next morning. Because she'd stayed up to finish her new comic, she'd slept late. Argh!

After leaping from bed, she dressed quickly, fed her snakes some dried peas and carrot curls from the snake snack sack she'd brought along, and then repacked her bag so she'd be ready to leave whenever Zeus returned for her and Dionysus. It never took her long to get ready in the mornings. That was one of the great things about having snake hair. It always looked good. Because snakes styled themselves!

As she went to leave her room, she noticed a folded papyrus note on the floor that had been shoved under her door. When she unfolded the note, she recognized Dionysus's handwriting right away. Eagerly, she began to read.

DEAR GREENIE-GIRL,

SILENUS HAS A MEGA-STOMACHACHE. OR

SHOULD I SAY "STOMACH-CAKE"?

"Oh no!" she murmured. But, really, no surprise
there, now that she thought about it. That goat had
eaten everything in sight last night. She read on:

I'M TAKING HIM BACK TO MY CHILDHOOD

HOME, SO THE NYMPHS CAN CARE FOR

HIM. THE SWEET GREEN GRASS FROM OUR

VALLEY WILL CURE HIM IN NO TIME. I

DIDN'T WAIT FOR YOU BECAUSE IT'S A

MAGICAL LAND WHERE MORTALS DARE

NOT GO. ZEUS WILL COME FOR YOU

TODAY OF COURSE. MEANWHILE, I'LL

STAY THE NIGHT, THEN CATCH A SHIP

ACROSS THE AEGEAN SEA AND BE BACK

AT MOA ON SUNDAY. SEE YOU THEN!

YOURS IN MAGIC,

DIONYSUS

"Ye gods, guys," she told her snakes. "We've been deserted." Her snakes drooped.

"I know how you feel," she told them. "I wish Dionysus hadn't gone off without us too. Sounds like it couldn't be helped, though. We'll just have to hang around with the king till Zeus arrives. It would've been way more fun riding back with Dionysus, but that's the way it goes." After lingering for a few moments over the words "Dear greenie-girl" and "Yours in magic," she refolded the letter.

As she slipped it into the pocket of her chiton, she remembered the wish Dionysus had granted the king the night before. "Hey, let's go see how that golden-touch thing is working out," she said to her snakes. Her step quickened as she opened her door to go find the king.

"Ye gods!" The sight that greeted her eyes made her gasp with wonder. The glitter of gold was everywhere in the cottage's living room. The chairs were gold. The floor tiles were gold. So was the table. And on the newly gold table was a gold platter piled high with gold apples, grapes, and peaches. These items alone had to be worth a fortune. The king was rich again!

The gold front door was standing open, so she figured the king must have gone outside. She stepped through the doorway and was mega-dazzled yet again. Because the entire garden with its rows and rows of rosebushes had been turned a shiny, gleaming gold!

"Beautiful!" she breathed. But then she heard someone sobbing. *King Midas?*

Medusa hurried through the sunlit rows of glittering gold rosebushes to find him. He was kneeling in front of a particular rosebush, now golden like all the others around it. It was near the also now-golden wicker tea table. And if she remembered correctly, this bush had been one of his favorites.

King Midas lifted his tear-stained face when he heard her approach. "Ruined. All ruined," he moaned. "I accidentally touched a single rose, and *whoosh!* The entire garden turned to gold."

"Oh." Medusa gazed around. "Probably because they were all connected by leaves or roots, I guess? But they're beautiful, don't you think?" She went closer to him, but then, thinking better of it, edged away again, so as not to get too close to his gold finger.

"No! They are *not* beautiful!" wailed the king. "Once, the roses on this bush were a deep ruby red with a scent like the finest perfume. And that one had orange roses, with a fragrance beyond compare. And that one over there was the violet-pink of a sunset. But now my poor rosebushes are all the same color and have no smell at all!"

Just then a bright yellow butterfly fluttered over to the king's favorite bush. Apparently not detecting any scent, it didn't bother to light on a rose to sip its nectar. She wondered if the shiny, metallic roses even *had* nectar now.

"True," she told him, "but just think. You can sell this whole lot and buy hundreds . . . no, *thousands* more of the normal kind of rosebushes to plant. You're rich!"

Crash! Turning, Medusa saw that Tanis had come

into the garden. Upon seeing the gold rosebushes, the girl had been so surprised that she'd dropped the tea tray she'd been holding. Before Medusa could speak to her, she ran off. How much of their conversation had she overheard?

"I nursed those rosebushes from cuttings!" the king said in a woeful voice, having hardly noticed the crash or Tanis. "They were my little rosebuds. My babies." He sadly cupped one of the roses nearest him in his palm. "I named this variety 'Sweet Child.'" Then he began pointing at another bush and another. "And that one 'Boy Wonder' and that one 'Pearly Girl.' Now I've destroyed them! I've destroyed them *all*. I wish I'd never made that wish!" he exclaimed. His eyes were filled with despair.

Then suddenly he leaped to his feet. "We have to do something to fix this!"

"Well, Dionysus said 'no take-backs,' remember? So I'm not sure . . ." Medusa began. She was positive that Dionysus had never anticipated this situation when he'd granted the king's wish. She certainly hadn't. As she tried to think what to do, she reached up to pat her snakes.

"I know, I know," the king said, nodding his head. "But shouldn't wishes come with some kind of 'satisfaction guaranteed' clause? That would make sense, wouldn't it? I can't be the only person ever to regret making a wish." A glint of hope came into his eyes. "As soon as Dionysus is out of bed, I'll ask him if there isn't some way to rid myself of—"

"Oh, but he's gone," Medusa hastened to tell him. She pulled Dionysus's note from her pocket and opened it, intending to read it to the king. But then she fumbled and dropped it. Without thinking, King

Midas reached to pick it up. As soon as his right index finger touched the note, it turned to gold.

"No big deal," Medusa assured him as he stared at the note in distress. It's still readable." It was true, for Dionysus's writing had become gold too, etched into the paper as if carved. As she stooped and picked up the note, she quickly explained that Dionysus had taken Silenus back to his childhood home and wasn't planning to return to Phrygia.

"If only someone else could lift this golden curse from my shoulders," the king moaned dramatically.

Medusa glanced around, mentally searching for an answer to this king-size problem. She couldn't believe that Midas wanted to get rid of the marvelous gift. Yes, you would need to be careful with it in order not to accidentally touch things you didn't want to turn to gold. But if you were cautious, like she was with her stoneglasses, surely it could be done. Why, having the golden touch was a gift worth its weight in . . . well . . . *gold!*

She was thinking that she'd trade her stone gaze for a gold finger any day, when she idly turned over Dionysus's note and noticed a P.S. that she had missed before. She skimmed the words he'd added:

P.S. IN CASE OF TROUBLE, PLEASE REMIND KING MIDAS THAT HIS WISH DOES NOT COME WITH TAKE-BACKS. THAT IS, NOT UNLESS SOMEONE IS WILLING TO TAKE THE WISH OFF HIS HANDS. AND THAT HAS TO HAPPEN WITHIN TWENTY-FOUR HOURS IN ORDER TO MAKE THE FINGERTIP-TO-FINGERTIP TRANSFER WORK.

"Godsamighty! That's it! I've found a way out of your wish," she told the king. She pointed to the note, and the king scrambled closer to read it. "Are you absolutely positively sure you want to be rid of the golden touch?" she asked the king. "Because if you do—"

"Oh, I do, I do," Midas interrupted her.

"Well, then I was thinking that you could transfer it to . . . *me*," Medusa said.

"But then *you'll* be stuck with it!" King Midas exclaimed, looking distraught again.

Stuck with the ability to create unimaginable riches? Ha! Medusa rolled her eyes. "It's a sacrifice I'm willing to make," she told him sincerely.

"If you're sure," Midas said hesitantly. "Think Dionysus's suggestion will really work?"

Medusa shrugged. "All we can do is give it a try.

87

Maybe first you should say out loud that you're giving your wish to me. Just to make it official." Then she quickly added, "And maybe say so in rhyme, since most magic spells are in rhyme."

"Okay." King Midas thought for a while. Finally he came up with something:

> *Please take my wish,*
>
> *If you would.*
>
> *I hope that it will*
>
> *Do you good.*

As his words died away, he reached his right hand out. Medusa reached her right hand out as well. Their fingertips inched closer. A split second before they touched, it occurred to her that she might have miscalculated. If so, instead of receiving the golden touch, she might be turned to gold herself! She didn't want to become a statue of gold here in Midas's garden today, thank you very much!

Too late! Before she could snatch her hand back or reconsider or even blink, their fingers met. That soft glow appeared—the one she remembered seeing when Dionysus had given the touch to the king.

Medusa hunched her shoulders, waiting anxiously to see what would happen. She'd actually become a marble statue once, when her own stony gaze had been boomeranged back onto her after Athena had tricked her into looking into a mirror. (Though, luckily, Athena had been able to remove the spell later.) So Medusa knew firsthand what the feeling of limbs turning stiff and cold was like.

She wiggled her arms and legs as though they were wet noodles, testing to see if she could still move.

Fortunately, that cold, stiff feeling she remembered from the other time did not come over her now.

The king's eyes widened, watching her in dismay. "What's wrong?"

She straightened, realizing she'd probably looked a little weird, wiggling all over. "Oh, nothing."

Looking relieved to hear it, the king suddenly ran over to an olive tree. He touched it, looking thrilled when it didn't turn to gold. "Now you try touching something," he told her, his eyes excited.

Just then a dandelion puff floated in the air past Medusa. "Okay. Here goes." She reached out, gently poking the puff with her fingertip. *Zing!*

Instantly the puff turned golden—and heavier. It dropped to the ground with a *clunk!*

At the same time a wave of color washed over the entire rose garden, restoring it to normal. The delicious fragrance of the roses filled the air around them once more.

"Not only did we transfer touches. We also reversed the effects of my original wish! Oh, thank you, thank you!" King Midas exclaimed. Kicking up his heels, he did an impromptu happy dance in the middle of the garden. And afterward he skipped from rosebush to rosebush, reaching to touch his favorite roses and bending to smell their heavenly fragrances before finally running off to the stone cottage. Medusa followed him inside and watched him zip around, gleefully noting that all the furnishings and other items had returned to normal, just as the garden had.

Hearing a mighty flapping sound, Medusa stepped outside again. She shaded her eyes and looked up to see Zeus and Pegasus coming in for a landing. She went to grab her bag, only remembering just in time to pick it up in her left hand, not her right. Then with a quick good-bye and thank you to the king, she scurried out the door.

She was sure Zeus would be impatient to leave right away, and besides, she didn't want King Midas spilling the beans about the golden touch. Zeus might not be exactly happy if he found out about the whole thing. And when he wasn't happy about something, he could get thundering mad! As in thunderbolts and lighting. Which could be very, very frightening! Not to mention loud and dangerous.

As Zeus hitched Pegasus to the chariot he'd left in the garden, she informed him that Dionysus was taking Silenus back to his childhood home and planned to board a ship back to MOA the next day. Zeus seemed to take this in stride and simply tossed her bag into the chariot, then offered her a hand up. Medusa quickly tucked her right hand into the pocket of her chiton and gave him her left, so she wouldn't turn *him* to gold. If that were even possible.

Putting her hand into her pocket caused her chiton to turn gold at once. But luckily, it stayed stretchy and soft instead of turning hard and rigid. Otherwise she wouldn't have been able to sit down in it.

Zeus appeared oblivious about the change to her chiton. He wasn't really looking at her, having already turned back to take up Pegasus's reins.

She was going to have to be very careful with this new ability, Medusa realized as Pegasus spread his golden wings and the chariot sailed into the sky.

She pulled her hand from her pocket and held her magic finger up in front of her face, staring at it. Excitement filled her. This was for real. She was going to be rich. Mega-rich. No more begging her sisters for money to do the slightest little thing. Why, she could sell this gold chiton for enough to live on for a whole year probably. She had that comic-scroll entry fee in the bag.

Sure, there might be a few pitfalls along the way with this whole golden-touch thing. But nothing she couldn't handle. Whatever trouble she might encounter, it was going to be way worth it!

6

Do Not Touch!

O**N THE FLIGHT BACK TO MOA, ZEUS ENTER-**
tained Medusa (and himself, mostly) by belting out
songs that had been sung in his honor during the
previous night's temple ceremony in Aizanoi. One of
them, his favorite apparently, since he sang it at least
six times, had lyrics that went like this:

Zeus is the mightiest god of them all.

In battle he is brave.

An incredible genius and great principal too,

The Olympians he did save.

So bow and tremble before his thunderbolts,

And never misbehave!

"It's just so *me*," Zeus told her each time he sang it. And each time, Medusa hastened to agree. After a little more than an hour had passed, they were landing in the courtyard at MOA. Medusa left-handedly grabbed her bag and jumped down from the chariot before Zeus could offer to help her.

"Thanks for the ride, Principal Zeus," she called to him as he unharnessed Pegasus from the chariot. She knew he'd spend at least an hour grooming and feeding his favorite winged horse before going inside. So with a quick wave she ran up the granite steps and escaped into the Academy.

Her golden chiton got a few curious stares from the students she passed on the way up the marble staircase to the girls' dorm, but fortunately her sisters weren't around to demand answers. Pheme and Pandora weren't either. Though the latter two were Medusa's friends, they were also nosy. She needed to think carefully about how, when, or even *if* she was going to reveal the news of her golden touch to them or anyone.

After making it safely down the hall to her room, Medusa set her bag on the floor so she could use her left hand to unlock her door. Since she was right-handed she had to fumble a bit with her key, but she eventually got the door open. Once inside, she tossed her bag onto her bed first thing, then relocked the door behind her.

Anxious to put her gold finger to use and try out her new superpower, she glanced around the room. Atop her desk sat a green feather pen preloaded with green ink; a nearly empty bottle of green fingernail polish; and a fist-size, ugly, lopsided ceramic pot with an ill-fitting lid that she'd made back in fourth grade Crafts-ology class. Perfect practice materials! She reached for the pot with her right hand. Naturally, as soon as she picked it up, the pot turned to gold.

Now it wasn't so ugly, though it was still lopsided. She took the lid off the pot and peered inside it. She'd expected it to be empty, but at the bottom she found a cheap bronze pin in the shape of a jellyfish and about the size of her thumb. She'd forgotten all about that pin!

"Hmm. Why didn't you turn into gold when I touched the pot?" she asked it, not expecting an answer, of course. Touching just one rose had transformed all the roses in King Midas's garden to gold. "There must be some logic to how this golden-touch stuff works," she said to herself. She hoped she'd figure it out sooner rather than later. Maybe Dionysus would have some clues to offer about the "golden" rules. *If* she told him what she'd done. He'd seemed reluctant to give the golden touch to Midas at first. How would he take the news that she had it now?

Reaching into the lopsided gold pot, she pinched the jellyfish pin between her right index finger and thumb and plucked it out. Before her very eyes the pin changed from dull bronze to a shiny gold. *Cool!* She remembered how in first grade she'd once used her meager allowance to buy this pin at the Obol Store back home, which sold lots of cheap knickknacks. Well, the pin wasn't so cheap anymore!

Setting the pin and the pot on top of her desk, she then picked up the feather pen next. As gold zipped over it, the feather stiffened and stood straight up. When she tried to write with it, being careful not to let her right index finger touch the paper, she found that the ink inside the pen had also turned to solid gold and the pen would no longer write.

Last of all, she touched the bottle of fingernail polish. Voila! Both the bottle and the polish within became a sparkly gold.

Taken together, all four items would fetch a pretty pile of drachmas in trade. And she knew just the store in the Immortal Marketplace where she could trade them. A certain greedy, tricky shopkeeper there owed her a favor and would doubtless prove willing to buy these objects.

Before unpacking her bag, she opened her closet

and groped around inside it with her left hand until she found a pair of fitted felt gloves. When she slipped the right-hand glove over her fingers, it turned gold. Luckily, like her chiton, it stayed soft and supple.

As a test she reached inside the closet again and poked an empty wire hanger with her gloved index finger. Success! The hanger did not change to gold. Which meant that the glove would keep her from accidentally turning other things to gold, until she could think of something more effective.

Medusa smiled to herself. Wearing this glove was sort of like wearing her stoneglasses. The former would keep her from turning objects to gold, while the latter kept her from turning mortals to stone. Controlling her golden touch was going to be a snap!

Humming to herself, she slipped off her gold chiton and hung it up at the back of her closet. Then she pawed through her other chitons, looking for one that wasn't too out of style or worn out. All of her chitons were green and, like so many of her other things, they were hand-me-downs from her sisters. Choosing the least shabby of them, a pale green knit whose hem was starting to unravel, she slipped it over her head.

"This will do for now," she told her snakes. "But once we get to the Immortal Marketplace and I make a trade for a pile of drachmas, I'll buy a whole *closetful* of new chitons if I want to. And some special treats for you guys too. First, though, I'm going to pay the fifteen-drachma entry fee for the Comicontest!"

Elated, she gathered up the nine comics she'd chosen the previous day, plus the new comic she'd drawn at King Midas's cottage. She put them inside her big green school bag, planning to take them all to the IM and deposit the comics in the contest box by the atrium. Lastly, she tossed in the gold pot, feather pen, and fingernail polish. She was about to add the jellyfish pin, but then she changed her mind and decided to keep it instead of trading it away.

After pinning it onto her chiton (which wasn't exactly easy with her right hand in a glove!), she grabbed a snake snack sack from her closet shelf and tossed a handful of dried peas and carrot curls to her snakes.

Snap, snap, snap! Given the speed with which they scarfed down the treats, they must have been ravenous. Which made sense. She was hungry too. None of them had had any breakfast! Deciding she'd wait and get something to eat at the IM, Medusa grabbed her school bag and was out the door.

As she started down the hall, she tried to figure out how she could get to the IM fast. Located halfway down Mount Olympus, the marketplace was far enough away that it would take several hours to walk there. Not fun.

Traveling by winged sandal would be ten times faster, but she couldn't operate the sandals by herself since she wasn't immortal. She'd have to be holding hands with a goddessgirl or godboy to make the sandals work. And whoever she asked to go with her would probably want to know why she was wearing a gold glove. She'd better start thinking of some good answers if she wanted to keep her golden touch hidden for a while.

"Yoo-hoo, Medusa, wait up!" someone called to her as she neared the door at the end of the hall. *Drat.* It was Pheme! As always, the orange-haired goddess-

104

girl's words were accompanied by cloud-letters that puffed above her head to spell out everything she said. Which meant that her words could be read far and wide. Being the goddessgirl of gossip, if she got wind of Medusa's golden touch, it would be all over the school in no time.

As Medusa hesitated near the door, Pheme caught up to her. She zeroed in on the golden-gloved hand right away. "What happened? Did you peek in Athena's diary?" she asked.

"Huh?" said Medusa. "What are you talking about?"

Pheme's hand flew to her mouth as if she'd just realized she'd almost given something away that she'd rather have kept secret. When cloud-letters echoing her words rose above her head, she brushed them away with both hands. "Oh nothing," she said in a fake-casual way. "It's just something I heard. That Athena keeps a spell on her diary. If anyone tries to read it, I, um, *heard* that the spell makes their hands turn red. Get it? So they're caught red-handed!"

Medusa stared hard at Pheme. "Mm-hm. I see." She'd have bet anything that this nosy girl had discovered the diary spell the hard way, by getting caught red-handed herself.

Interesting. And since the brainy Athena wouldn't just leave her diary lying around, Pheme must have snooped in her room to find it. This made Medusa extra glad she kept her door locked, unlike most students. She shifted her gaze to Pheme's hands, wondering how she'd managed to remove the red-hand spell.

Noticing, Pheme stuffed her hands in her pockets.

"I was just going to the cafeteria to get some lunch," she said as they went through the hall door and started down the marble stairs together. "Want to eat with me? You can tell me about your trip with Dionysus and Principal Zeus. Might make a good article for my column in *Teen Scrollazine*." Pheme had been writing a gossip column for the scrollazine for some time now.

"I've got a better idea," Medusa said, having a sudden brainstorm. "I'm on my way to the IM to do some shopping. If you go with me, I'll treat you to lunch there." Pheme was immortal, plus she had *wings*. So Medusa might not even need the winged sandals if Pheme came with her.

"Really?" Pheme's brown eyes lit up, and her small orange wings fluttered at her back. "I'd love to go."

"Will I . . . um . . . need winged sandals?" Medusa asked uncertainly as the girls reached the main floor and started toward the Academy's bronze front doors. She eyed the communal basket of sandals by the exit. Pheme had only had her wings for a short time—they were a reward from Principal Zeus for an act of bravery—and Medusa hadn't flown with her since she'd acquired them.

Pheme shook her head. "My wings have magic that's strong enough to keep two aloft. But you'll still need to hold on to my hand." She glanced curiously at Medusa's gloved hand again.

"I've got a . . . um . . . skin condition," Medusa improvised quickly. Seeing Pheme's look of horror, she added, "Don't worry. It's not contagious or anything."

"Oh, I wasn't worried," Pheme said. But from the

relief in her voice, Medusa knew her friend was fibbing.

After the two girls pushed through the door, Medusa tactfully offered Pheme her ungloved hand to hold. Then they were off to the marketplace, where they arrived in hardly any time at all.

7

Shopping Spree

THE IMMORTAL MARKETPLACE WAS BEAUTIFUL

and enormous, with a high-ceilinged crystal roof.

Medusa kept a tight hold on her green schoolbag as

she and Pheme walked between the rows of columns

that separated the various shops. Here you could buy

pretty much anything your heart desired. And that

included the newest Greek fashions at clothing stores

such as the Green Scene, as well as tridents, spears,

and athletic equipment at Mighty Fighty, which (not surprisingly) was every godboy's favorite store.

The girls paused briefly outside Arachne's Sewing Supplies, where the window held an enticing display of colorful yarns, ribbons, and fabrics, before continuing past Cleo's Cosmetics. Walking on, they passed Demeter's Daisies, Daffodils, and Floral Delights, a plant shop owned by Persephone's mom. It was from her that Persephone had inherited her green thumb.

"Want to eat at the Hungry, Hungry Harpy Café before we go shopping?" Pheme suggested, gesturing toward the restaurant a few doors down.

Medusa had never been out to eat in the IM ever. She couldn't afford it. Until now. "Sure!" she told Pheme. "Definitely." There was plenty of time to trade in her gold and enter the Comicontest too, after lunch. And she was starving!

"Ooh! Awesome! I've heard they test customers' wits by trying to sneak off with the food they serve them."

"That's weird," said Medusa, frowning. But Pheme wasn't listening. As the girls came even with a pet supply store called Ship Shape, the gossipy girl asked, "Have you ever been in that place? It's fantastic!"

Medusa glanced toward the pet store's blue door. "Just once. They only sell stuff for birds and fish, though. Not snakes." Still, it was a cool store. Inside was a freshwater pool! You entered on a gangplank that rested on pontoons and led to the ship that served as the store. Actual fish swam in the pool, and birds flew in and out of the hole in the roof above the shop.

The Hungry, Hungry Harpy Café was within sight now. It was just past the gift store with the blabby gift box puppets that had landed Medusa in hot water a while back by alerting guards to her snakes' wedding gift shoplifting attempt.

While Pheme was looking ahead to the café, Medusa glared at the gift store puppets as she walked past them. Her snakes hissed at them too. The puppets nearest the window went round-eyed in surprise and alarm after all. Humph! They deserved it. They'd sounded the alarm. So it was pretty much their fault she'd ended up having to clean her sisters' room a gazillion times in exchange for Stheno and Euryale keeping her and her snakes out of trouble.

Upon reaching the café, Medusa and Pheme grabbed the H-shaped door handles and entered. The walls and ceiling inside were decorated with secondhand items including an antique violin, some rusty farm equipment, paper fans, and sparkly costume jewelry.

Pheme elbowed Medusa gently in the side. "Think they stole all this stuff to bring here?" Her excited words puffed above her head for anyone to read.

Instinctively Medusa clutched her bag to her chest. She hadn't remembered that Harpies had a reputation as pickpockets and thieves, or she never would've agreed to come here. If they found out she had a bag full of gold, would they try to steal it? She swiped a hand through the air, dispelling the cloud letters. "Shh! Tone it down. Don't draw attention to us," she urged Pheme.

A Harpy waitress hurried over to the two girls. Even though the Harpies were the goddessgirl Iris's sisters, they looked nothing like Iris, and had much larger wings than her more delicate ones. "Come in, come in," the waitress said, her broad wings flapping at her back. "Have a seat at the counter. We've just started to serve

114

lunch. Can I bring you two blue-plate specials?"

Pheme and Medusa looked at each other uncertainly. Since neither of them had actually eaten here before, they had no idea what the food was like. "Sure," Medusa answered for both of them. They'd just have to hope they liked whatever they were served. At the counter the girls seated themselves on cute stools made from old leather trunks. Medusa held her bag on her lap, taking no chances.

She had slipped on her stoneglasses as soon as the girls had landed at the IM. Now she peered through them at a gray-haired old man who was seated on a stool farther down the counter. As he reached for a cup of coffee, a second Harpy waitress appeared out of nowhere. She swooped down on him and yanked his half-finished plate of a sandwich and chips off the counter.

"Give that back!" he yelped as she hurried off with it. "You know I wasn't done eating!"

"Now, Phineas," cooed a third Harpy. "You wouldn't keep coming back if you didn't like the service. Right?"

The old man muttered something that sounded like, "Darn thieving Harpies!" Then he wrapped both his gnarled hands around his coffee cup as if he feared the waitress might return to take that, too!

"Keep an eye on your plate," Medusa cautioned Pheme as the first waitress returned and set their blue-plate specials—delicious-looking fish and chips with a side salad—in front of them. It was good advice, only Pheme didn't heed it.

When a bell over the café's door jingled a few seconds later, the nosy girl turned her head to see who the new customer was. Instantly one of the Harpy waitresses who'd been hovering nearby reached out and snatched a few fries from Pheme's plate.

"Hey," Medusa protested, grabbing the Harpy's arm in her gloved hand before the waitress could steal any more. Clueless, Pheme was still staring over her shoulder at the customer who had just come inside, probably trying to figure out if it was someone famous and worth interviewing.

"Nice glove," said the Harpy, eyeing its shiny, gleaming fabric. "Is it *real* gold?"

"Do I look like I could afford real gold?" Medusa replied cagily. As the Harpy's gaze swept the old hand-me-down chiton she wore, Medusa tightened her other hand's hold on her green bag, adding, "Hey! I think that customer over there is calling you."

With a cackle the waitress moved away. Having totally missed out on what had just happened, Pheme turned back to her food. Maybe she'd concluded that the customer wasn't anyone famous after all.

"Eat up," Medusa told her. "I've got lots of shopping and other stuff to do." And that stuff included entering the Comicontest. Her comic-scroll collection and the contest fee had to be in the entry box by sundown.

There was another reason for her to hurry, too. She didn't trust those Harpies not to somehow steal her glove right off her hand! Even now they were all three whispering together and eyeing it. If they did steal it her gold-making finger would be exposed, and that could lead to disaster if she accidentally touched something. The sooner she and Pheme were outta there, the better.

Luckily, the café soon became crowded, allowing the girls to finish their specials with no further interference from the Harpies, who were kept busy filling orders and snitching food from other customers. Medusa paid for both her meal and Pheme's, using the last of her allowance. Until she sold some gold, she was broke! She breathed a sigh of relief when they made it back out the café door with her glove still on her hand, and her bag over her arm.

"Mind if I run back over to Cleo's Cosmetics?" Pheme asked right away. "I need a new tangerine lip gloss." Orange was her favorite color. Any shade.

Perfect, thought Medusa. She'd needed an opportunity to ditch Pheme for a while so she could run her errands in secret. "Sure, go on," she said. "I'll do a little window shopping and meet you back at Cleo's in a few." It wasn't exactly a lie. Because once she had some cash, she would shop till she dropped!

As soon as the girls separated, Medusa hurried

over to Mr. Dolos's Be a Hero store. It sold all kinds of products such as drinking mugs and posters with autographed pictures of mortal heroes on them. She'd vowed never to have any dealings with the slimy shopkeeper again after he'd tricked her into letting him put a scary-looking picture of her head on some shields he'd sold in his store. But now she had need of him.

The short round man behind the store's counter paled a bit when she came up to him. "Hi, Mr. Dolos." *Thunk!* Medusa set her green bag on the counter.

Nervously running a hand through his slick, black hair, Mr. Dolos peered beyond her. "That godboy friend of yours isn't with you, is he?" he asked anxiously. He was wearing the same bright yellow-and-black-checkered tunic he'd been wearing the last time she'd seen him. Or maybe not the same one. He probably had a whole closetful of those tacky tunics!

Medusa grinned, knowing that the shopkeeper was referring to Dionysus. After she had told him how Mr. Dolos had tricked her, Dionysus had brought this guy back to MOA stuffed in a mail sack so he would have to face Medusa and her accusations.

"Not at the moment," she replied. Wouldn't hurt to let him think that Dionysus was shopping somewhere nearby in the mall right now.

She opened her bag. One by one she set the gold pot, the gold feather pen, and the bottle of gold fingernail polish on the counter. Seeing them, Mr. Dolos's eyes glittered as brightly as the items, maybe more. His large, dark mustache twitched with greedy excitement as he asked, "And just how did you come by these?"

"They're not stolen, if that's what you're thinking.

And never mind where I got them," she told him. "Just tell me how much you'll give me for them."

He looked the three items over, gauging their weight in the palm of his hand. Then he bit down on the pen, presumably to test if it was real gold. "Fifteen drachmas," he said finally. It was an absurdly low figure, and they both knew it.

"Ha!" she snorted. "Try adding a zero to the end and making it one hundred and fifty." Was it too much? She wasn't sure, but she was determined to make a better bargain with him than she had the last time.

"Twenty," he countered.

"*One hundred* and twenty," she shot back.

"Thirty drachmas and not a penny more," he said stubbornly.

Medusa glared at him. "I don't have time for

this! I've got to meet my *friend* in a few minutes. So what's your best and final offer?" she demanded. She hadn't lied, since she did need to get back to the makeup shop to meet Pheme, but she hoped that the shopkeeper would think she was speaking about Dionysus.

Mr. Dolos tugged nervously at the neck of his checkered tunic. "You drive a hard bargain, but all right, then. One hundred drachmas."

Was that good? Medusa wondered. Who cared? It was good enough! And she could always make more gold objects to sell whenever she needed to. She was rich! So she nodded. "It's a deal."

Mr. Dolos counted out the coins and placed them in the palm of her golden-gloved hand. If he wondered why she wore just the one glove, and how come it was as gold as the objects she'd just sold him, at least he didn't ask her any questions about it.

With the hundred new drachmas safely stowed in her bag, Medusa hurried to the center atrium before going to meet Pheme. Next to a splashing fountain in the midst of some magical rhododendron bushes that bloomed with flowers all year round, she found the box for the Comicontest entries.

Following the directions printed on a sign above it, she took an envelope from a holder attached to the box, scribbled her name on it using the pen provided, and then put the required fifteen-drachma fee inside. It had taken her way longer than normal to write with her left hand, but she'd managed it.

After sealing the envelope, she tucked it under the ribbon she'd tied around her comic-scroll collection. Then she deposited her collection inside the box, which was so stuffed with entries already that she could barely fit hers inside.

"There!" she congratulated herself. "Done and done!" Now she'd just have to hope for the best. Considering there were so many other entries, the competition could be stiff.

Thinking about the eighty-five drachmas still in her bag, she practically skipped on air the whole way to Cleo's Cosmetics. There she found Pheme in the process of paying the shop's purple-haired, three-eyed owner for lip gloss as well as a few other items she'd picked out.

"I'm going to look for a new chiton at the Green Scene. Want to help me choose something?" Medusa asked as the girls left Cleo's. The Green Scene sold only green clothing. Stheno and Euryale shopped there all the time, but it had always been too expensive for Medusa. Until now, that was.

"Woo-hoo! Somebody must've just gotten an increase in her allowance," Pheme said, grinning at her. Medusa just shrugged happily, letting her think she was right. Pheme looped an arm through Medusa's, adding "Sure. C'mon."

As they neared the Green Scene, Pheme pointed to a kiosk across the way. "Look, there's Hermes." Wearing winged sandals, a winged cap, and a long tunic, he was just leaving with an armload of packages. The Hermes' Delivery Service kiosk was a new addition to the IM. It sold packaging supplies such as envelopes and boxes, and you could leave packages there for later delivery.

"Looks like he's off to his chariot to make more deliveries," said Medusa. Hermes and his package-filled, silver-winged chariot were a familiar, daily sight at the Academy. Though he was always grumpy about taking on passengers, she had hitched a ride in his delivery chariot several times.

Once the girls got to the Green Scene, Medusa tried on several chitons, all of them the newest style with sleek lines and flowing skirts. As she modeled them for Pheme, her friend oohed and aahed over them all, unable to decide which she liked best.

Medusa's snakes were able to give her a bit more feedback, however. They hissed at the chitons they didn't like when she looked in the shop's full-length mirror, but bobbed up and down excitedly when she modeled one they thought looked especially good on her.

After trying on ten outfits, Medusa narrowed her selection to five. "They're all cute," Pheme agreed. "So which one will you get?"

Medusa frowned. "I don't know." She checked the prices. Then slowly she smiled. "I think I'll get all of them," she said. And why not? The chitons were on sale. And besides that, she now had the means to buy everything she wanted, no matter what the price! So she also picked out pretty green ribbons for all of her snakes. There was nothing orange for Pheme, or Medusa would've gotten her something too.

Feeling deliciously happy, Medusa took the chitons and the ribbons over to the counter. *I'm riding high now!* she thought. She had entered the Comicontest and hoped to win. And she had plenty of money and the means to get more. People were fond of saying that money couldn't buy happiness, but they were wrong in her opinion—because money was making her mighty happy right now!

As the Green Scene clerk was ringing up her purchases, the bell over the shop door rang. Medusa's smile froze in horror as her two sisters walked in. Instantly their eyes fell on the pile of drachmas she was holding out to the clerk and all of the chitons spread over the counter.

"Who died and left you a fortune?" grumped Stheno, coming over.

"Yeah," echoed Euryale. "Or did you just rob a bank?"

8
Trade-Offs

H A!" MEDUSA SAID TO HER TWO SISTERS, GIVING

a fake laugh. "Me robbing a bank? Very funny." But

inside her chest a panicky feeling was growing. As

she finished paying the clerk, she tried to think of

a convincing story to explain her newfound pur-

chasing power. Her sisters knew just how small her

allowance actually was. They knew there was no way

on Earth or Mount Olympus that she could've saved

enough to pay for those chitons, even on sale.

Meanwhile the clerk was bagging her purchases. And Pheme was listening intently, probably hoping for some good gossip she could spread.

"Well?" asked Stheno, tapping her foot impatiently. "Where did the money come from?"

Out of nowhere a good answer came to Medusa. "Mr. Dolos," she announced. Which was the truth, of course. "He owed me some royalties for using my picture on those toy shields he made a while back, remember?"

This was also true, except Medusa had turned down the hundred drachmas in royalties he'd once tried to pay her because she'd been so disgusted at what he'd done with her image. He'd used it to scare people and had claimed the shields were magic when they weren't!

Seemingly satisfied with her answer, her sisters lingered nearby awhile longer. "Why are you wearing that glove?" Euryale asked as Medusa reached for the bag of five new chitons, which the clerk was now holding out to her.

Pheme piped up. "She's got a skin disease." The words puffed from her lips to hang in the air above her.

The clerk, who hadn't seemed fazed by Medusa's snakes, now gave a little gasp and took a step back.

"A skin *condition*," Medusa corrected quickly. "And it's not contagious. Just a bit of dryness and some flaking. That kind of thing."

Stheno grinned at Euryale. "Maybe she's molting," she joked. "Shedding her skin just like her snakes."

Euryale laughed gleefully. "Yeah. That's got to be it!"

Though her snakes hissed, acting annoyed on Medusa's behalf, Medusa was happy to let her sisters have their little joke. It was better than them finding out the truth about her golden touch. "Right," she said in a perky tone. "You got it in one!"

"Really?" said Pheme, her eyes rounding in surprise. This cracked Stheno and Euryale up anew.

"No. They were joking," Medusa explained patiently.

Stheno snorted. "Or maybe not. See you both back at MOA!" she called over her shoulder as she and Euryale headed farther into the store to look for clothes themselves.

Phew, thought Medusa. *Talk about a close call!*

When she and Pheme arrived back at the Academy a half hour later, Medusa said a quick good-bye and hurried to her room. After carefully hanging her new chitons in her closet and stashing her leftover drachmas in the back of her desk drawer, she decided to go do something she loved as much as Artemis loved archery. Swimming! Having grown up on the coast of the Aegean Sea with a sea monster for a mom and a sea hog for a dad, Medusa was a natural at it.

In fact, she'd learned to swim almost before she could walk. And if earlier in the year some nasty sea nymphs hadn't pushed her five-year-old kindergarten buddy into the school pool during a swimming race—thus necessitating a rescue—Medusa would have won that race. And she'd have also secured the right to accompany Poseidon down the aisle as a bridesmaid during Zeus and Hera's wedding.

Not that she minded in hindsight, she thought as she changed into her swimsuit and a cover-up and grabbed a towel. If she hadn't played the hero and rescued her buddy that day, Dionysus might not have become her friend and crush. And he was a much worthier friend than Poseidon, in her humble opinion.

Heading for the gym, she passed several students when she crossed the courtyard outside, but beyond a quick wave or a "Hello," they left her alone. Which was just the way she wanted it at the moment. Out on the sports fields groups of students were heaving spears, shooting arrows at targets, and climbing up and down rope nets. More Temple Games practice.

Once inside the gym, she took the limestone stairs two at a time down to the pool below. As godboy of the sea, Poseidon had created this underground pool and many others around Earth and Mount Olympus. He sometimes magically changed this pool's shape for special MOA events. He'd made it heart-shaped for Zeus and Hera's wedding, for example! And sometimes he added waterfalls, rocks, and various fishy creatures too.

Today the pool was its usual rectangular shape,

though, with braided sea grass ropes marking off the swim lanes. Medusa looked around as she pulled off her cover-up and towel and set them aside. Luckily, she was the only one there. She loved the times when she had the pool all to herself.

Without thinking, she pulled off her glove and reached out to test the water's temperature. As soon as her index finger grazed the surface of the water, she realized her mistake. She jerked her hand back. But it was too late. Already, gold sparkles raced across the pool, turning the water into something that resembled a huge golden butterscotch pudding.

Medusa could only watch with alarm and regret as the golden "pudding" began to harden into solid gold. Quickly, she shoved her hand back inside her glove. Just why liquids should harden, while cloth stayed flexible, she wasn't really sure. She only knew she was helpless to do anything about it! When she heard the basement door open, she threw on her cover-up. Several voices rang out, and footsteps clattered down the limestone steps, coming closer.

Hide! her brain screamed. She grabbed her towel and looked around wildly. Spying a large basket for wet towels a short distance away, she raced over to it. After removing its lid, she jumped inside, finding it empty. Quickly she covered her head with her towel and lowered the lid into place.

Just in time! Seconds later she heard a voice she recognized as Pandora's call out, "Hey, what happened to the pool?"

"It's gold!" another girl shouted in astonishment. Was that Iris? Medusa wasn't sure, and she didn't dare lift the lid to peer out, in case someone saw her. She kind of wished she hadn't hidden. She probably could've bluffed her way out of this, pretending the pool had been gold when she'd arrived. But now it would look suspicious if she leaped out of this basket. And even more suspicious if someone found her in here. Argh!

"Think this is Poseidon's doing?" asked a third girl.

"Why would he want to make it so no one can swim here?" Pandora asked dubiously.

"It's kind of pretty, though," said the girl Medusa thought might be Iris. "But rainbow-colored would be even prettier."

Definitely Iris. Medusa hunkered lower inside the basket until she finally heard the girls leave. Then she waited another few minutes before she climbed out and headed back to the Academy. Along the way she avoided eye contact with the students she passed, hoping no one would take notice of her swimming

138

outfit and eventually put two and two together.

No doubt the whole school would soon be buzzing over the mystery of the golden pool, she thought as she climbed the marble stairs to the dorm. She shuddered to think what might have happened if anyone had already been *in* the pool when she'd touched the water. Thank godness no one had been!

With luck Poseidon would be able to change the hardened gold back to water without too much trouble. He was an immortal, after all. He could perform *real* magic. He wasn't limited to the occasional quasi-magic of a stony gaze or a golden touch the way she, a mere mortal, was.

As she slipped inside the dorm hallway—thankfully empty of girls at the moment—she tried to think of ways to waterproof her right index finger so she'd be able to swim if Poseidon ever managed to fix the pool. Sadly she faced the truth. That there was no way she could ever go swimming again, not even if she wore her glove or wrapped her finger in something else. She'd always worry that the water from the pool would leak through and the whole pool would turn to gold again.

And the next time, someone else might be swimming. And maybe they would be turned to gold. What a horrible mistake that would be. *Ye gods!*

Once back in her room, Medusa flung her unused towel onto her bed. To ease her disappointment about not being able to swim, she decided to try on all the new chitons she'd bought at the Green Scene again.

Each time she modeled a different one before the mirror that hung on the inside of her closet door (while wearing her stoneglasses, of course), her snakes got caught up in the excitement. They did themselves up in various hairstyles—from braids, buns, and fancy chignons to spikes, twists, and crazy updos—all to complement her outfits. They were probably also trying to cheer her up after what had happened at the pool, she guessed. And it worked.

"Thanks, guys. This golden-touch stuff is trickier than I thought it would be," she admitted to them as she dug into their snake snack sack and tossed them dried peas and carrot curls. *Snap! Snap! Snap!* The treats were gone in an instant.

"I should have figured there would be trade-offs, like not being able to swim," she went on as she put away the snacks. "But it's worth it, right? Just think, I'll never have to worry about money again." She wasn't sure who she was trying to convince more— her snakes or herself.

Seeming to sense her doubt, Wiggle and Sweetpea

dropped their heads to nuzzle her cheek. The sweeties! She knew they were trying to reassure her that all would be well.

Greatly cheered, she asked her snakes, "So, do you think I should wear one of my new chitons when Dionysus gets back tomorrow?" She felt all twelve snakes bob their heads up and down in approval of the idea. But for now Medusa reached into her closet for the same old chiton she'd worn to the IM.

"He's going to be curious about my glove," she murmured as she slipped the knitted green chiton over her head. "I won't be able to lie to him about my so-called skin condition. He'll guess the truth. Especially once word gets around about the solid-gold pool. Think I should admit what happened? That King Midas regretted the golden touch right away and passed it on to me?"

Again her snakes all nodded. After a pause, she nodded too. "Okay, but let me pick the right moment to make my confession. Don't give me away," she told them.

Just then someone pounded on her door. "Open up," Stheno called out.

"Yeah," echoed Euryale. "Don't keep us waiting."

With an irritated sigh Medusa let them in.

"You lied to us," Stheno accused right away.

Medusa tensed up. "About what?" she asked, trying to make her voice sound casual. Had they found out about the pool and guessed about her golden touch?

"That wasn't royalty money Mr. Dolos gave you," Euryale put in, wagging a finger in Medusa's face.

"Yeah," said Stheno. "You sold him some stuff made of gold. He showed it to us."

Euryale frowned at Medusa. "And we want to know where you got it."

Rats, thought Medusa. It had never occurred to her that her sisters might check out her story. Conscious of her golden glove, she clasped her hands behind her back.

Suddenly Stheno's eyes darted to the pin on Medusa's chiton. "Hey, I remember that jellyfish pin!" she exclaimed, poking a finger at it. "But it wasn't *gold* before!"

"You've got some explaining to do, Sister," Euryale said, getting in her face. Carefully keeping her hands behind her, Medusa took a step back.

"Yeah," said Stheno. "'Cause we don't believe for a second you've got a skin disease. Why are you really wearing that glove?" Before Medusa could stop them, her sisters each made a grab for one of her arms.

"Stop! Wait!" Medusa cried out, wriggling away. She was worried they'd pull off her glove. As awful as her sisters were, she didn't want to turn them into gold statues!

They backed off. "Go on, talk," said Euryale. "Only, you'd better tell us the truth this time."

"All right," said Medusa, feeling cornered. "If you're going to act like babies about it, I'll tell you what you want to know. But you have to swear an oath of mumness about what I'm going to say."

"Deal," her sisters said quickly. With any luck, they would actually keep quiet about her new ability—at least for a while. They were better at keeping secrets than Pheme, anyway. So Medusa told them all about her golden touch, how she'd acquired it, and about making the gold items she'd sold to Mr. Dolos.

A calculating gleam came into the two girls' eyes

as she was speaking. "Do you think you could get Dionysus to give us the golden touch too?" Euryale asked after Medusa had finished her story.

"Doubt it. He doesn't even know I have it yet," Medusa reminded her. "He bestowed it on King Midas as a reward for his kindness and hospitality to Dionysus's pet goat, remember? What have you two ever done for Dionysus?"

"Nothing," Euryale admitted. "I'd sure like to know what kind of spell he used, though. I've never been able to do any get-rich-quick magic. Hardly anyone can."

"I wouldn't want to have to cover up my finger all the time anyway," Stheno said to Euryale. Then she cocked her head at Medusa. "So whenever we want money, we'll get *you* to turn something to gold for us. Okay, Snakehead? After all, you owe us. Think of all the things we've done for you over the years."

"Hmm." Medusa folded both arms and cocked her head thoughtfully. "I'm trying to."

"What? Don't forget how we helped you trick your way into enrolling at the Academy back at the start of third grade," said Stheno. "And over the years we've stood up for you when other kids tried to bully you or your snakes."

"True. But you also bully me yourselves," challenged Medusa. "'Snakehead' isn't the nicest nickname you could think of. And you call my snakes nasty names too. And, oh, by the way, if I do give you a single gold thing—and I'm not saying I will—that would be the end of me cleaning your room. Debt paid."

To her surprise, both sisters nodded eagerly.

"And if you ever did tell anyone about my golden

touch, you'd have to repay me any of the gold or money I'd given you," added Medusa.

Stheno crossed her heart. "It'll be a family secret."

Euryale nodded in agreement. Then she held out her hand palm upward and wiggled her fingers meaningfully. "Now how about sharing some of those drachmas you got off Mr. Dolos?"

"Why should I?" Medusa protested. "You and Stheno just got your allowance, and it's three times more than what I get."

Stheno snorted. "That's only because Mom and Dad love us more."

She hadn't meant it as a joke, and it wasn't one. Their parents had made it clear Medusa's whole life that, compared to her two immortal sisters, she was a huge disappointment to them.

Euryale rolled her eyes. "Thing is, we already

spent all our allowance at the marketplace. And what's the big deal anyway? You can always make more gold, which equals more money to spend."

Her sister had a point. "True," Medusa said. Caving at last, she stepped over to her desk and slid open the drawer. Then she reached in the back of the drawer for her remaining drachmas. The five chitons had been on sale for eight drachmas apiece, and the dozen ribbons had cost another four drachmas altogether. Along with the fifteen-drachma contest fee, that meant she'd spent fifty-nine of the hundred drachmas Mr. Dolos had given her.

She divided the remaining forty-one drachmas, giving twenty to each of her sisters and only keeping one for herself. "But be careful, okay? If you go crazy spending this and whatever I give you later on to buy all kinds of stuff, people will start to ask nosy questions. Like you just asked me!"

"You worry too much, Little Sister," Stheno said, slipping the drachmas Medusa had given her into her chiton pocket.

"Yeah," said Euryale, doing the same. "Wanna go buy some snacks and shakes at the Supernatural Market?" she asked Stheno.

"Sure," said Stheno as she opened Medusa's door so they could leave. "I'm thinking *bags* of snacks, and maybe three or four shakes apiece."

"Yeah! Why not?" Euryale said as they started into the hall. "We've hit the jackpot!"

Medusa shut the door behind them. "Obviously they didn't understand a word I said," she grumbled to her snakes. "And did you notice how they didn't even ask me to go with them to the market? Not that I wanted to, but still."

Her snakes curled around her neck and lightly flicked their tongues to show their sympathy. She patted them with her gloved right hand, then switched to her left—because petting her snakes with a glove was not nearly as satisfying as touching them with bare fingers. And that was something she'd never be able to do with her right hand ever again.

9
Family Matters

WHEN MEDUSA WOKE UP SUNDAY MORNING,

she was startled to see that her glove was on the floor.

It must have fallen off during the night somehow

while she'd been asleep. Luckily, she'd slept with her

arm flung over the side of the bed, her hand touch-

ing nothing but air, or she might have turned her

bedcovers to gold. Or maybe even herself! She still

wasn't totally sure how the golden touch worked and

wasn't about to try it on herself, lest she become a statue again.

Being careful not to touch the floor, she reached down and picked up the glove. As she slipped it back over her right hand, she vowed to tie a ribbon around the bottom of it at night from now on to make sure it stayed on.

She fed her snakes first thing, tossing handfuls of dried beans and celery curls high into the air. "Good morning, Viper, Flicka, Pretzel, Snapper, Twister, Slinky, Lasso, Slither, Scaly, Emerald, Sweetpea, and Wiggle," she called out to them as they snatched at the snacks and gulped them down.

She wished she could take a shower, but that seemed out of the question. Instead she settled for a bath in the bathroom down the hall. While carefully keeping her right arm dangling outside the tub, she washed left-handed. It wasn't easy and took a lot longer, but at least she didn't turn herself, the water, or the soap to gold!

She'd just gotten back to her room when she heard a sound at her window. *Tap. Tap. Tap.* When she opened it, in whooshed a magic breeze. *Letter delivery,* it announced, immediately dropping a letterscroll tied with a silver ribbon. Medusa caught it in her golden glove. "Thanks," she called as the breeze whooshed away.

"Think it's from Dionysus, maybe?" she said to her snakes as they leaned forward for a better look at the scroll. She hoped he wasn't writing to say that his goat was still sick and he'd be delayed in returning to MOA. She untied the silver ribbon and began to unroll the letter:

To: Medusa Gorgon

From: Big D Publications

A flutter of excitement shot through her. *Ye gods!* Big D Publications was the sponsor of the Comicontest! The competition had only just ended yesterday, so Big D was certainly fast in responding. Especially given the large number of entries that had been stuffed into the contest box. Was it possible she'd won? Taking a deep breath, she unrolled the rest of the letterscroll:

Congratulations! You have been selected as the Grand Prize winner of the Big D Publications Comicontest!

155

"Woo-hoo!" she whooped, before eagerly reading on.

To complete the prize award

process, please come by our offices

at your earliest convenience.

Big D Publications

Suite 142, Immortal Marketplace

Prize award process? That probably just meant she'd need to sign a contract before her comic collection could be published, she decided. Where was suite 142? she wondered next. Did all of the shops in the Immortal Marketplace have numbers? If so, she'd never noticed them.

"Guess this means another trip to the IM," she said, doing a quick happy dance around her room. "But who cares, right?" she said to her snakes. "My comics won! I am going to be published. Yeah!"

If Dionysus got back early enough today, maybe he could go with her to the IM so that she wouldn't have to ask Pheme or her sisters to take her. As excited as she was about winning the contest, she'd never shared her comics with anyone before. She could hardly wait for Dionysus, especially, to read them in print!

Excited beyond belief, Medusa hurriedly dressed in one of her brand-new chitons, a hunter-green one made from a soft fabric with a scalloped hem. After unpinning her gold jellyfish pin from her old knit green chiton, she fastened it to her new chiton. Then she wound one of the twelve green ribbons she'd bought yesterday around each of her snakes. After slipping on her stoneglasses, she and her snakes preened in front of the closet mirror. Her snakes were so pleased with their appearance that she practically had to drag them away from their reflections to go to breakfast.

She kept her stoneglasses on as she started down the hall. Wearing them was pretty much second nature by now, since several mortals attended MOA, including Pandora, who was just now leaving her room. Athena, Pandora's roommate, was with her. The two girls fell into step beside Medusa. "You and your snakes look extra nice today," Athena said, smiling at Medusa's hair ribbons.

Medusa's snakes drew themselves up a little taller and prouder at the compliment. "Thanks," said Medusa, "on behalf of both me and my reptiles."

Pandora eyed Medusa's glove. "Pheme told me about your skin disease?" she said. Making a statement sound like a question was something the curious girl often did. "Is it a rash?" she asked next. "Does it itch? Will you have to wear that glove forever?"

Medusa shrugged, which was sometimes the best way to answer all of Pandora's questions at once. She and Pandora had actually been roommates for a short time, and after that, Medusa had roomed with Pheme briefly. But Pandora's constant questions and, later, Pheme's constant chatter and resulting cloud-letters had driven Medusa crazy.

So she'd turned Pandora's questions back on her and established a no-cloud-letters ban with Pheme that had eventually rid her of first one roommate and then the other. Really, she much preferred rooming with just her snakes. They were not only good company; they were *quiet*.

Perhaps because Pandora had drawn attention to Medusa's glove, Athena kept glancing at it.

Remembering what Pheme had said about the red-handed spell on Athena's diary, Medusa wondered if this brainy girl was suspicious of her now. Well, if Athena wanted to believe that Medusa had snooped in her diary and was covering up the result with a glove, maybe that was better than her knowing the truth . . . for now, anyway.

In the cafeteria Medusa snagged a plate of ham-brosia and eggs from the eight-armed lunch lady and went to sit next to Pheme, who was already at their usual table. Stheno and Euryale were seated there too. They were too busy whispering to each other to pay any attention to Medusa, though.

Pheme chattered on about this and that, cloud-letters rising above her head, but Medusa was only half-listening. Instead she was thinking about how great it was going to be to see her comics published, and about all the things she could buy now that her golden touch would guarantee her an endless source of wealth.

Maybe she'd buy her very own chariot, she mused. Then she'd never again have to ask anyone for help using winged sandals. She'd have to convince Zeus to let her keep a chariot at MOA, though. So far he'd only allowed Artemis to do that. Hers was pulled by milk-white deer with golden antlers. But Medusa thought it would be cool to have sea serpents pull hers.

Suddenly a loud grunting noise sounded from over by the cafeteria door, causing a hush to fall over the students.

Medusa gave a start. *Huh?* She'd know that sound anywhere! Like everyone else in the cafeteria, she glanced toward the door. Ye gods! Her worst suspicions were confirmed. There stood her dad, Phorcys, a sea hog who only talked in gruntspeak. And next to them was her mom, Ceto, a sea monster. What were they doing here? she wondered. They'd never come to MOA before. Not even for special occasions!

Her parents gazed around the cafeteria, and within moments her mother's eyes zeroed in on her. "Dusa!" she exclaimed. "My baby!" Like a nightmare come to life, she waddled across the room and enveloped Medusa in a big hug, right in front of all the other students.

What? Her mother *never* hugged her.

Medusa was so embarrassed, she wanted to sink right through the floor. She wished her mom had just ignored her, same as always, and gushed over her sisters like she usually did instead. What in Zeus's name had gotten into her?

Her dad had slithered on over too, grunting away.

Now he was smiling down at her, his fish tail flopping back and forth across the floor behind him.

"Umm. Why are you guys here?" Medusa couldn't help asking. She glanced over at Stheno and Euryale. "Did you know Mom and Dad were coming?"

Her sisters shook their heads, but a guilty look passed between them. Then their mom said to Medusa, "After we got your sisters' special delivery letterscroll last night, we decided to just show up and surprise you! Our little golden girl!"

Special delivery letterscroll? Golden girl? Oh, great. *Just great,* thought Medusa. *Not!* So her loose-lipped sisters had been unable to keep her secret for even one day. Instead they'd immediately gone and spilled the beans to their parents. And since her parents normally didn't have any time to spare, their visit could only mean one thing. They wanted to exploit her new ability. Sure enough, Ceto began to hint around about the additional rooms and the swimming pool she and Phorcys had always wanted to add on to their small cottage back home.

Tossing her sisters a dark look, Medusa began trying to coax her parents outside the cafeteria. "We should talk somewhere more private," she said, managing a smile. Her mom and dad allowed her to lead them outdoors and across the courtyard. She was taking them toward the olive grove, where they'd have less chance of being seen or heard.

Along the way they passed the school's new anemometer, a gadget used to measure wind speed. The anemometer had been combined with the carved likenesses of the four winds—Boreas, Zephyr, Notus, and Eurus—by the amazing sculptor Pygmalion during monstrous Typhon's recent rampage, the same rampage that had destroyed King Midas's palace and the homes and farms of the people of Phrygia!

"Show us how your wonderful new magic works," her mom insisted eagerly as soon as they were inside the grove.

With a heavy sigh Medusa withdrew her glove. After dropping it onto a bench at the center of the grove, she demonstrated her golden touch on a couple of ordinary rocks she picked up. Pleased with the result, her parents scouted around for more rocks, and a couple of sticks, too. These Medusa also turned to gold.

Her parents loaded a bag they'd brought from home with the gold rocks and sticks. "Thanks, Dusa," said her mom. "This will do for now. We'll let you know when we need more." Then, after a grunt from her dad and a murmured farewell from her mom, the two of them headed for home.

"Aren't you going say bye to Stheno and Euryale before you leave?" Medusa called in surprise.

Ceto turned her head and smiled. "We really only came to see you," she called back.

"Uh-huh," her dad grunt-agreed. Then the pair slithered and waddled on down the trail that would take them to Earth.

Medusa had often dreamed of hearing her mom or dad say such loving words to her. But their words rang hollow now. They'd only come because she was finally able to give them something they really wanted. Gold!

Once her parents reached the sea, they'd probably swim home—or take a ship if their bag of gold proved too heavy—she thought as she watched them disappear from view. She'd always wished her parents would pay her more attention, but not in this way. Not because they simply wanted her to give them money!

Medusa picked up her glove from the bench and slipped it over her right hand again. "It'll be a *family* secret," she remembered her sisters promising. They'd tricked her, of course, but she couldn't exactly accuse them of breaking their promise, since their parents *were* part of their family!

Whoo! Whoo! Just then a big brown owl swooped down from the tree above her head to land on the bench where her glove had been resting just moments before. Then, right before her eyes, the owl transformed into a brown-haired goddessgirl with blue-gray eyes.

"Athena?" squeaked Medusa. "Um, how much did you see?"

10

Keep-Away

EVERYTHING," SAID ATHENA. "I SAW AND HEARD everything. Sorry for spying, but you were acting so suspicious earlier, and—"

"Pheme told me about your dumb diary," interrupted Medusa. "I never touched it," she added in a prickly tone of voice. "Believe it or not, I don't make a habit of prowling around in other people's rooms." The words came out sounding angrier than she'd intended.

Mainly because she was embarrassed that Athena had overheard what had happened with her parents.

"I believe you." Athena easily brushed aside her argumentative comments, then motioned for Medusa to sit on the bench beside her. "I'm guessing you weren't expecting your mom and dad to show up at school. Parents can be so embarrassing, right?"

Medusa sat, sighing. "That's for sure." Athena could undoubtedly relate to parent problems. Her *real* mom was a fly named Metis who'd already buzzed off by the time Zeus had met and married Hera. Having Zeus as a dad couldn't be easy either. He could be loud and corny. And since electricity shot from his fingertips whenever he got angry, he probably sometimes zapped Athena's friends . . . and maybe even her crush, Heracles. That would be mega-embarrassing.

Athena hesitated, then nodded toward Medusa's glove. "This golden-touch business is bad news," she said in a more serious tone.

"Not for me it isn't," Medusa replied defiantly. Athena really *had* heard everything! Feeling cornered, Medusa jumped up from the bench and began to pace back and forth in front of it.

Athena raised an eyebrow. "Maybe it doesn't seem like such a bad thing right now, but sooner or later you'll regret it."

"Doubt it," Medusa muttered stubbornly.

"So how did it come about, anyway?" Athena asked curiously.

Still pacing, Medusa explained, adding that Dionysus didn't yet know that King Midas's golden touch had been transferred to her.

When Medusa was done, Athena pursed her lips

in disapproval. "Dionysus should have known better than to grant such a wish," she said. "He should have tried to dissuade Midas from his foolish choice."

"I don't think it was so foolish," huffed Medusa.

"Well, if my dad finds out about it, he won't be happy," Athena told her. "And when word gets out, which it's sure to do eventually, it'll be an even bigger disruption than . . . than . . ."

"Than the one Ares' sister Eris caused when she came here to MOA?" Medusa finished wryly.

Eris was the goddessgirl of strife and discord. When she'd shown up at Ares' birthday party not long ago, she'd proceeded to divide the school in half and pit students against each other in an academic contest had raised grades for a time, but had resulted in strained friendships and major fights. As leaders of the two opposing contest teams, Athena and Aphrodite had been right in the middle of the whole mess.

Athena had the good grace to blush at the reminder. "Point taken. But you will think about what I've said, won't you?"

Medusa nodded. Besides being the brainiest goddessgirl at the Academy, Athena was also the goddess of wisdom. So her ideas were often worth listening to.

"So, when will Dionysus get back?" Athena asked as she and Medusa left the grove and entered the courtyard. Lots of students had finished eating breakfast by now and were standing around hanging out with friends, or sitting on benches to read or study.

"Sometime this afternoon, I'm guessing," Medusa replied. "He's sailing back." She noticed that students shied away from her as she passed by. Had Pheme spread the news about her so-called skin disease? If so, it looked like she'd forgotten to add that it wasn't contagious.

"Going back inside?" Athena asked when they reached the granite steps leading up to the Academy's front doors.

"Uh, not right now," Medusa replied. It had just occurred to her to wonder if Poseidon had been able to fix the pool yet. Deciding to wander over and find out for herself, she said bye to Athena and started toward the gym.

As she approached the sports fields, she realized something. Athena had issued a warning to her about the golden touch, yet she hadn't really offered a *solution*—that is, a way to get rid of it. Maybe that meant there *wasn't* a way to get rid of it now that the short window of time for passing the touch on to someone else had closed. No matter. Medusa didn't *want* to get rid of her golden touch!

She'd just started across the sports fields toward the gym when she nearly got clobbered by a badly thrown ball. Two godboys named Makhai and Kydoimos came running toward her as she scooped up the ball in her gloved hand.

These godboys were occasional friends of Aphrodite's crush, Ares, with well-deserved reputations as bullies. Instead of apologizing for almost hitting her (typical!), the beefy-looking Kydoimos merely asked, "What's up with the glove?"

"Haven't you heard?" Medusa said archly as she handed the ball back. "I have—" But before she could finish telling him that she had a horribly infectious skin disease and that the two boys would be wise to keep their distance, a grinning Makhai reached over and whisked her glove off.

"Hey, give that back!" Medusa yelled in a panicky voice. But the two boys just laughed. Immediately they began to toss her glove back and forth in a game of keep-away.

Medusa raced after her glove, trying to catch it as it sailed between Makhai and his friend, first one way and then the other. However, the boys always managed to toss the glove just high enough to be out of her reach. Just when she was about to explode with frustration, the glove dropped lower.

She reached overhead with both hands to nab it. Unfortunately, her snakes chose that exact moment to help out. Just as Medusa reached, they wiggled, stretching high with their mouths open to snag the glove. Her ungloved fingers brushed against one of them.

Instantly her snakes went still. A heavy weight settled on top of her head.

"Oh no!" she wailed. Stoneglasses still in place, she ran to a nearby fountain and stared in horror at her reflection in the water at the base of the fountain. All twelve of her snakes had frozen mid-wiggle. And they'd turned to gold!

Makhai's usually squinty eyes widened. "Whoa!" He pointed to the top of her head. "Your snakey hair just became a snakey gold crown!"

"Awesome," said Kydoimos. He reached to pick up Medusa's glove, which had fallen to the ground between him and Makhai.

"It's *not* awesome!" snapped Medusa. She wondered why she hadn't been turned to gold too, but for some reason the change had only come over her snakes. Maybe because they weren't exactly part of her? They were themselves, her pets. At least they had been.

Now she truly, deeply understood how King Midas must've felt when his roses had turned to gold. He'd loved them just as she did her snakes! Feeling sick at heart, she burst into tears. Then, unable to help herself, she sank to the ground, sobbing.

Makhai and Kydoimos exchanged looks of horrified discomfort. Though skilled at bullying and, in certain classroom situations, at cheating, too, a crying girl was apparently more than they could handle.

Despite it being much too late to matter now, Kydoimos handed Medusa her glove. "Sorry," he said.

Without a word Medusa pulled it on. Brushing tears from her face, she rose and started back to the school, still sniffling. Her feet felt like they were encased in heavy lead. And bowed down with grief and a permanent golden crown, her head felt like it weighed a ton. Her original mission to check on the pool was totally forgotten.

Makhai grabbed the ball he and Kydoimos had been tossing around earlier, and the two boys trailed along after her.

She whirled around. "Stop following me! I'm dangerous. Don't you get it? One touch of my finger, and I can turn you to gold too!"

The boys flinched back for a moment. Then, as complete understanding dawned, they caught up to her again. Makhai squinted at her and held out their ball. "How about turning this to gold for us, huh? There are a couple of things I've been wanting to buy at Mighty Fighty, but I'm kind of short on funds, and—"

With a strangled cry Medusa raced away from the boys. Ignoring the stares of other students, whose eyes fastened in wonder on her golden snake crown, she ran up the granite steps of the school, pushed through the bronze doors, and practically flew up the marble staircase despite her heavy head.

Luckily, no one was in the dorm hall as she dashed to her room. Once inside, she flung herself onto her bed and wept for her poor snakes, who were now quite unable to comfort her.

As Medusa lay there sobbing, she was startled by a rapping at her window. *Tap. Tap. Tap.* For the second time that morning, a breeze had brought her a letterscroll. She untied the ominous black ribbon around it and fumbled to unroll it with her gloved hand. Finally she got it open:

Yo ho ho!

If ye want to see Dionysus again,

bring a hundred pieces of go-ho-hold

to our ship right away, hey, hey! I'm

sure King Midas will supply it!

—The Pirate King of Melos

P.S. Tell no-ho-ho one else.

P.P.S. Come alo-ho-hone.

On the back was a rough drawing of a map marking the location of the pirate ship in the middle of the Aegean Sea.

Medusa stood there for a few seconds, totally stunned. Could this day possibly get any worse? Only now did she remember the pirate ship Dionysus and Zeus had flown over in the Aegean Sea on their way to Phrygia. Were these the same pirates Zeus had thrown a thunderbolt at? Who knew? There were lots of pirate ships plying the Aegean.

Well, whatever this pirate king's fame and power, he was definitely behind in his news. King Midas wouldn't be able to meet their demand for gold because *she* was the one with the golden touch now, not him.

Did Dionysus know that somehow? Is that why he'd apparently told the pirate king to send this ransom letterscroll to her? Nearly crazed with fear for Dionysus and grief for her snakes, Medusa thrust the letterscroll into her pocket. Knowing she had to try to rescue her crush, but having no plan for how to do that, she raced down the hall toward Athena's room.

The few girls she passed in the hall nudged each other and pointed at her head, staring wide-eyed, but she ignored them. When Athena came out of the bathroom just then, her hand flew to her mouth as she stared at Medusa's golden snake crown. "Oh no!"

"Oh yes," said Medusa, panic gripping her. "And it gets worse."

Athena tugged her across the hall into her dorm room, then closed the door behind them. "Sit!" she ordered, pointing to Pandora's bed. So Medusa sat. "Pandora's hanging out with Pheme, so we can talk freely. Now, take a deep breath, then tell me everything."

Medusa's panic eased some after the deep breath, but her heart was still pounding as she pulled out the pirate king's letterscroll. Her hands shook as she passed it to Athena without another word.

Athena scanned the letterscroll quickly, frowned, then handed it back. "Melos is the name of an Aegean island famed as the refuge of pirates. So the

Pirate King of Melos is probably pretty powerful. But I still don't get how he could keep an immortal like Dionysus a prisoner. Pirates are mortals. That god-boy can do magic. He should be able to escape."

"I know," said Medusa. "I don't understand it either. Should I use my golden touch to pay the pirates' ransom? You know, turn a bunch of stuff to gold that they could then sell?" she suggested anxiously.

"Let's ask my dad," Athena said right away, as Medusa had supposed she might. But then the brainy girl clicked her tongue in annoyance. "Only, he's not here. I just remembered that he and Hera went off to another temple celebration this morning. And I don't even know where they were going!"

A teeny part of Medusa was relieved that she wouldn't have to face Zeus with all this. Not yet, anyway. But mostly she was upset that he was gone, because she was sure she'd need his help to rescue Dionysus. "Well, I have to do something. Maybe I can pay Hermes to take me to Melos in his chariot. That is, if I can find him."

Knock, knock. Athena's door opened, and Artemis and Aphrodite stuck their heads in. "We were just going down to the—" Aphrodite started to say, but she fell silent when she caught sight of Medusa's golden snake crown.

"What's going on? How did that happen? Is it permanent?" Artemis spluttered. With all her questions, she sounded like Pandora! As the two girls came inside, Medusa and Athena quickly filled them in on everything.

"I can't sit around and wait for Principal Zeus to get back." Medusa dashed for the door they'd left open. "I've got to go to Dionysus's rescue. Now!"

"Stop!" Athena exchanged a meaningful glance with Aphrodite and Artemis. Then Aphrodite came over and touched Medusa lightly on the shoulder. "You shouldn't go all by yourself. Let us come with you."

"All right," Medusa agreed.

"We can take my chariot," Artemis said as the four girls started up the hall.

"Or my swan cart," offered Aphrodite as they made their way down the marble staircase together. "It's smaller than the chariot, but it's actually faster for long-distance travel."

"Then let's take the swan cart, please," said Medusa. Although she still felt low, their support was buoying her spirits a little.

While Aphrodite ran back upstairs to her room to grab her cart, the other three girls continued on down. The students they passed all turned to stare at Medusa's golden snake crown. Out in the courtyard Makhai and Kydoimos had apparently wasted no time in informing everyone—with or without Pheme's help—about Medusa's golden touch. A few students crowded around her now, holding out objects they wanted her to turn to gold.

"Go away," Athena scolded them. "Shoo! This is a tragedy, not a moneymaking opportunity."

"Yeah," said Artemis. "Medusa loved her snakes as much as I love my dogs."

Medusa gulped. *Loved* her snakes. Past tense. Could her snakes ever be brought back to life again? she wondered. Her heart felt broken in two. Or in twelfths. One sad part per snake.

Athena and Artemis linked their arms through Medusa's and powered their way past everyone—the curious, the sympathetic, and those asking Medusa for favors. When the girls came upon Apollo, Artemis hurriedly asked him to feed and walk her dogs while she hung out with her friends for the rest of the day.

"No problem. Glad to," Apollo replied. Then, looking at Medusa, he said, "Sorry about your snakes. I know how close you are . . . I mean, uh, *were* . . . to them."

"Thanks," murmured Medusa. Of course she and her snakes had been close. The snakes had grown from the top of her head, so she didn't see how they could have been any closer. There just *had* to be a way for them to return to life. If not, she didn't know how she would bear it!

Once Aphrodite caught up with the rest of them, she stooped to place a small ceramic figurine on a marble tile in the middle of the courtyard. The intricately designed figurine showed two swans side by side, pulling a golden cart behind them. The swans' faces were turned toward each other. With their orange beaks pressed together and their necks gracefully curved, they formed the shape of a perfect heart between them.

After stroking a fingertip over the swans' snowy white backs, Aphrodite stepped back, chanting:

"Feathered swans, wild at heart,
Spread your wings to fly my cart!"

The two swans fluttered, shaking their heads as if awakening from a deep sleep. Then slowly they began to unfurl their wings while growing larger and larger. By the time their wings were fully spread, the swans had become ten feet tall! Each with a wingspan of twenty feet. The small golden cart had grown along with the swans and was encrusted with splendid jewels that sparkled in the sun. It was now big enough to comfortably seat all four girls.

Was there a chant that could bring her snakes back to life in the same way that Aphrodite's chant had made her swans come alive? If so, then Medusa silently vowed she would search to the ends of the Earth and Mount Olympus to find it!

Aphrodite petted her swans' long, curved throats. "Ready?" she asked the others. They all nodded, then hopped aboard.

"To the Aegean. Up and away!" Aphrodite called out. Immediately the swans' brilliant white wings began to flap, and they rose gracefully above the courtyard, pulling the golden cart behind them. After gliding smoothly over the top of the five-story

Academy, the swans stretched their necks straight out in front of them and sailed southeast, setting a course for the coastline.

Thinking about all that had happened that morning, and what might lie ahead, Medusa's head bowed under the weight of her sorrows and worries, not to mention the weight of her golden snake crown.

She desperately hoped that if they were able to rescue Dionysus, he'd somehow be able to take away this golden *curse* and restore her snakes to life. Because now she had to admit that Athena had been right. The golden touch was *very* bad news, and Medusa had come to utterly regret making that deal with King Midas!

11

Searching for Pirates

APHRODITE'S SWANS SAILED OVER THE COAST
and were soon flying above an expanse of shining blue water. The girls peered over the sides of
the cart at the little islands that dotted the waters
of the Aegean Sea here and there. In and around
the islands were lots of ships. From high in the
air they looked as tiny as the thumb-size model
ships MOA students sometimes moved around a

three-dimensional game board in Mr. Cyclops's Hero-ology classes.

Medusa pulled her stoneglasses from the pocket of her chiton and put them on. She also withdrew the ransom letterscroll. Flipping it over, she and Artemis, who were sitting together in the backseat of the cart, consulted the sketched map the Pirate King of Melos had made to mark the location of his ship.

"If the pirate ship is still in the same area this map shows, it should be a little ways past that group of islands we're passing on the left," noted Artemis.

"Can you get your swans to go lower?" Medusa shouted to Aphrodite, who sat in the front seat of the cart by Athena.

"Sure." Aphrodite called back. Moments later the swans swooped closer to the water. Several ships were sailing nearby. The first one the girls flew alongside proved to be a trade ship, however. The sailors aboard it stared in awe at the goddessgirls—and at Medusa's golden snake crown. Meanwhile, the captain informed the girls that the ship was carrying wares such as woven cloth, pottery, and olives.

"Ye gods! I never imagined that my invention of the olive would become so popular that it's now an item of trade!" Athena said with excitement as they flew on.

The next ship they came to was a tour ship ferrying a group of sightseers from island to island. A man with a megaphone was speaking to the tourists on board. "And if you'll look up and slightly to our right," he told them, "you'll see a swan cart carrying a group of goddessgirls off the starboard side of the ship."

"Ooh! Aah!" chorused the awestruck passengers.

A few of them whipped out pens and pads of papyrus to quickly sketch drawings of the swan cart and its illustrious occupants. Aphrodite laughed, but Medusa was taken aback by the attention. They weren't some pod of dolphins frolicking in the sea for people to gawk at, for godness sake!

"So, what's our plan for when we finally find the pirate ship?" Artemis asked as they left the tour ship behind.

"You'll drop me off," Medusa said. "The pirate king said to come alone."

Aphrodite shot her a quick, worried glance from the front seat. "I don't think that's such a good—"

"I'm the only one who can supply the ransom," Medusa interrupted to add. She held up her gloved right hand meaningfully. "After I turn a few things to gold, I'm sure they'll let Dionysus go."

Athena turned around in her seat. "But what if they don't? What if they try to capture you, too?"

Medusa pointed to her stoneglasses. "No problem. I'll just whip these bad boys off and turn them all to stone!"

The other girls gasped, but then Athena said, "Well, if it has to come to that . . . as a last resort—"

"And only if extreme measures are necessary—" added Aphrodite.

"Then do what you have to do," finished Artemis.

While they continued to hunt for the pirate ship, Aphrodite, Athena, and Artemis pumped Medusa for more details about her visit to Phrygia. Were they just trying to keep her mind off her worries? she wondered. Whatever the reason, the distraction helped.

When Medusa described King Midas's rose garden, everyone immediately thought of Persephone, agreeing that she would have loved to see it. "Too bad she's at home for the weekend with her mom. She'll be disappointed she didn't get to come along to help us," said Artemis.

After searching the sea for more than an hour, they were beginning to wonder if they'd ever find the right ship. But then Medusa spotted one a little outside the search area that had grapevines running up its masts. "Look! That's got to be it," she said excitedly.

The other three girls stared. "What makes you so sure?" asked Athena.

"See those grapevines curling up the ship's masts?" Medusa said matter-of-factly. "Dionysus is god of the grape, right? I'm guessing he caused those vines to grow as a signal to me that he's on board that ship."

"Smart thinking!" said Athena.

Medusa smiled, though she wasn't really sure if Athena's remark had been directed at *Medusa's* smarts or at Dionysus's smarts.

As they approached the ship, Medusa realized she had a bit of a problem. "Uh-oh. Just remembered I can't swim anymore." She pointed at her snakes. "Too heavy. I'll sink. Maybe even drown." Not to mention she might possibly turn the entire Aegean Sea to solid gold like she had the MOA pool! "Can you guys hover low and long enough for me to climb down the side of the cart onto the ship's deck?"

Aphrodite nodded. "I think so."

Before dipping closer to the ship, Athena cast a spell over the swan cart to keep the pirates from seeing them:

"Cart, fly us all unseen below.

One, two, three. Ready, set, go!"

As the swans dove toward the ship, Medusa studied the layout of its deck. "After I've rescued Dionysus, we'll take down the grapevines as a signal that we're ready for you to pick us up," she told the others.

"Okay," Athena agreed. "But in the meantime, as a precaution, we'll try to find my dad. Just in case it turns out we need his help."

"And if the grapevines aren't down in an hour, we'll come after you regardless," Artemis added.

With that settled, the invisible swans swooped so low that the girls could feel the sea spray. When they were only a few feet above the ship, Medusa clambered over the side of the cart and dropped onto the deck.

The pirates on board were busy at various tasks, pumping out the seawater that constantly leaked aboard any wooden ship, scrubbing the decks, and mending sails and ropes.

Medusa tiptoed across the deck. Score! She reached Dionysus without anyone noticing her. He was sitting with his back to her, his hands around a mast, his wrists lashed together with rope. She tapped him on the shoulder, whispering, "Shh, it's me."

"Medusa?" He whipped his head around to look at her. His violet eyes widened as he took in the golden snake crown on top of her head. "What happened?" he gasped. "And where's Zeus?" he asked, craning his neck to look beyond her. "When I told the pirate king to send his note to you, I expected you would take it to Principal Zeus."

"He wasn't around," Medusa told him quickly. "So

I came in an invisible cart with Athena, Aphrodite, and Artemis. They're off looking for him now."

"But your snakes!" he said, his eyes going to the top of her head again. "Did King Midas accidentally touch—"

"No," Medusa shook her head, then almost toppled over at the shifting of the unaccustomed weight of the snakes. She showed him her gloved hand. "He didn't want the golden touch after all, so he transferred it to me." She felt her face cloud up. "I thought I would like it, but now I only wish I could get rid of it too." Then, forcing a smile, she said, "But at least it'll give me the power to pay your ransom!"

Suddenly one of the pirates glanced their way. "Hey! Who are you? What are you doing here?" he yelled, dropping the sail he'd been mending. And just like that, Medusa was discovered.

The ship's crew surrounded her and Dionysus, their eyes glued in greedy wonder to her golden snake crown. In short order the pirate king was informed of her presence, and he came down from the ship's bridge to confront her.

She hadn't expected him to look so noble and handsome. He was dressed in a clean white tunic and a dashing sky-blue cloak, and his curly brown hair hung to his shoulders. Below a finely chiseled nose he sported a neatly trimmed mustache and beard.

"I've come to pay the ransom to free your prisoner," Medusa declared.

Twirling the ends of his mustache, the pirate king looked around suspiciously. "Are you alo-ho-hone?" he asked.

"Yes," Medusa assured him. If the situation

hadn't been so dangerous, she might've giggled—because he talked just like he'd written his letter, with all that ho-ho stuff.

His eyes went to the top of her head. "Good," he said. "Give me that unusual golden snake crown of yours, and we'll let you and Dionysus go-ho-ho free."

Dionysus glared at him, but the glare was wasted, since the pirate king wasn't looking his way.

Though her heart was beating fast, Medusa said calmly, "Sorry. Not possible. Even if I wanted to give it to you, I couldn't." She hesitated for a moment. "You see," she said, "it's attached." She pulled gently on the golden snakes to prove it.

A flash of surprise came over the pirate king's face, but it was soon replaced by a cruel smile that made him look considerably less handsome. "No-ho-ho problem," he said, shoving aside his sky-blue cloak to reveal the gleaming sword at his side. "I can just chop off your head!"

"How dare you even *suggest* such a thing!" shouted Dionysus. "If I had my full powers right now, I'd—" His words petered out. In frustration he tugged his bound wrists against the mast, as if hoping to saw through the rope.

"Pipe down!" the pirate king snarled at him.

"Why can't you use your magic to free yourself?" Medusa whispered to Dionysus.

"Didn't you know?" he whispered back. "Whenever I use my magic to grant a wish, my powers are weakened for three days afterward. These pirates captured me after I took my goat home and was on my way back to MOA. I couldn't fight them with magic. After giving King Midas the golden touch, I barely had enough magic left to run these vines up the masts."

The pirate king took a menacing step toward them. "Stop that whispering!"

"Here's the deal," Medusa told the pirate, eyeing his sword with trepidation. "You can't have my crown, but I'll give you all the gold you want. *After* you release Dionysus."

The pirate king folded his arms, lifting a skeptical eyebrow.

She pulled off her glove. "Don't believe me? Here, I'll show you." She reached out with her right index finger and touched a coiled length of rope that lay nearby. Immediately gold sparkles zipped around and around the entire length of the rope coil, turning it to bright gold.

"Amazing! Wow! We're rich!" marveled the pirates. Several of them sprung forward to touch the golden rope. One even lifted the end of it to his mouth and bit down to test that it was real gold.

Medusa slipped her glove back on. "Well?" she said to the pirate king.

He cocked his head. "Mind-blow-ho-ho-ing!" Then he nodded toward the two biggest and burliest members of his crew. "Seize her!"

Before Medusa could think what to do, the pirates had bent her arms behind her back and tied her hands together, which made it impossible for her to remove her glove to turn them to gold—or to take off her stoneglasses to turn them to stone!

Shaking with fury, Dionysus shouted, "You let her go, you . . . you rotten, disreputable pirates!"

"No-ho-ho way," the pirate king told him calmly. "But don't worry. I've decided not to chop off her head after all. With that go-ho-holden touch of hers, she's worth far more to us pirates alive than dead."

Twirling his mustache again, he turned back toward Medusa. "One thing confuses me, though-ho-ho. How did *you* get the touch? I'd never even heard of it until I read about it in the latest *Fierce Pirates Periodical*. The article said a certain King Midas had acquired it."

So that's where he got his information about King Midas! thought Medusa. She'd been sure that Dionysus wouldn't have told the pirates about the king, so she'd been wondering. But how had the *Fierce Pirates Periodical* gotten wind of the information? Not from Pheme this time. She'd been far away at MOA, not anywhere near Phrygia on Friday and Saturday, when the whole golden-touch wish had happened.

Then, in a flash, the answer came to her. *Tanis!* It must've been her. King Midas's cook had seen the golden rosebushes, and maybe the gold things inside the cottage too. And she'd overheard Medusa and King Midas talking about the golden touch. She must've told everyone in the village, and then word had somehow spread to a writer for the *Fierce Pirates Periodical*. And Tanis had run away before Midas had transferred the golden touch to Medusa, so she hadn't known about that.

Medusa saw no harm in explaining to the pirate king what had happened, so she did. At the same time she began shaking her head from side to side, trying to dislodge her stoneglasses. But they stubbornly refused to budge from the bridge of her nose.

"What do you mean, no-ho-ho?" demanded the pirate king.

"Er, I didn't say 'no,'" Medusa said in confusion.

Had he asked her a question that she'd somehow missed while concentrating on trying to remove her stoneglasses?

"Then why were you shaking your head?" the pirate king asked.

"Oh. That. Um, my glasses are pinching my nose," she lied. "I was trying to shift them."

The pirate king rolled his eyes. "Somebody help her out," he said.

Huh? He and his gang must not know about her stone gaze, Medusa thought in surprise. Awesome!

A pirate with a hook on the end of his arm instead of a hand reached over and snagged the glasses off her face.

"Aha!" she said in triumph as her stoneglasses clattered to the deck. "Now you'll get what you deserve. I'll turn you all to stone!" She whipped her head this way and that, staring ferociously at the pirate king and his crew. But nothing happened. Her stone gaze wasn't working!

"Your ability to turn mortals to stone must have been bound up with your snakes," guessed Dionysus.

Or maybe she'd lost it when she'd first gotten the golden touch, thought Medusa. Either way this was bad news.

"Ho-ho-ho!" laughed the pirate king. "You'll turn us to sto-ho-hone, will you?" He picked up her stone-glasses and set them back on her face. "I like your swagger, girl. So I'm adding you to my crew. As long as you do as I say, you and grapevine boy are safe. Which means that whenever I ask you to turn an object into go-ho-hold, you do it. Now, welcome aboard! You'll learn to like it here after a year or two."

Before he left for the bridge, he ordered the two burly pirates who had bound her hands behind her back to secure her tied wrists to a heavy spool of rope. She was truly stuck now. She wouldn't be able to move around the ship.

Medusa was mortified that her plan had gone so wrong. "I'm sorry I flubbed your rescue," she whispered to Dionysus when the pirates had all gone back to their work. At least they could still talk, since they'd been left facing each other, seated only a few feet apart.

Dionysus sighed. "Not your fault. Besides, my powers will return in a couple more days and then we'll be outta here."

"A couple more days?" But what about her snakes? She wanted them back to normal as soon as possible. *If* possible. She scanned the skies. "Athena,

Aphrodite, and Artemis said they'd come looking for us an hour after they dropped me off. If they've found Zeus, they'll bring him."

"If only I had my full magical powers!" Dionysus lamented. His hands balled into fists of frustration. "Then none of this would have happened and we'd both be back at MOA."

"You said your magic is weakened for three days after granting a wish," said Medusa. "What does that mean exactly?"

"It means for another day and a half, I can only do the smallest, simplest spells, like running grapevines up ship's masts. I can't do any magic strong enough to free us," Dionysus replied. Then he added, "But I can help your snakes."

"You can? How?" Medusa asked, perking up.

"Shh," said Dionysus. He cocked his head toward

a peg-leg pirate who had just appeared. They waited until he'd stumped by before they continued talking. "I had a feeling King Midas might change his mind about his wish," Dionysus explained. "So as I was taking Silenus back home, I filled a vial of water in the Pactolus River. Its waters are magical and can undo the effects of unwise wishes."

She saw one of his arms move against the mast he was lashed to and knew he must've touched the curly vine on it with his bound hands. Instantly a piece of vine unwound itself from the mast. "Get the vial from my pocket," he commanded the vine. Obediently it snaked into his tunic pocket and snagged the vial. Then Dionysus directed the vine to open the vial and shake drops of water over the top of Medusa's golden snake crown.

And voila! Medusa felt one of her snakes wiggle.

Then another. Then a dozen as all of her snakes wriggled back to life.

Overjoyed, she called each of them by name in soft, delighted tones. "Viper, Flicka, Pretzel, Snapper, Twister, Slinky, Lasso, Slither, Scaly, Emerald, Sweetpea, Wiggle! I've missed you all so much!" Her snakes snuggled up to her, curling and uncurling along her neck and cheeks.

"I think they're happy to see you again too," Dionysus said with a grin.

Suddenly Medusa got an idea. "Flicka, Slinky," she whispered, "take off my glasses, please." When the snakes obeyed, curling around the glasses and pulling them away, Medusa tried an experiment. There was a pile of fresh fish lying in the middle of the deck only a few feet away. She stared into one of the fish's eyes. Instantly the fish turned to stone. "Sorry about that, buddy," she murmured. The fish had been destined to become the pirates' dinner soon anyway, but she still felt she should apologize.

Dionysus had been watching her experiment. He and Medusa exchanged a meaningful look as Flicka and Slinky replaced her glasses on her face again.

"Excuse me, Mr. Pirate King!" Medusa called out loudly. "There's something over here I think you ought to see!"

12

Riches

WHAT IS IT?" THE PIRATE KING CALLED OUT irritably. *Stomp! Stomp!* He left the ship's bridge again to make his way down to Medusa. "You think I have nothing better to do than keep coming o-ho-ver here? You think it's easy running a pirate ship? It's not all plundering temples and ships and ho-holding passengers for ransom, you know-ho-ho. Our course has to be carefully navigated, the ship needs constant repairs, supplies and water have to be brought in, and . . . huh?"

Abruptly he froze, a look of astonishment on his face. Because he'd finally noticed that Medusa's golden snake crown had been replaced by live writhing snakes! Which were doing their best to act menacing by flicking their tongues and hissing at him and his crew.

"*Sooo-ho* sorry," Medusa told the pirates sweetly, though she wasn't really sorry at all. "It seems I've lost my golden touch." She smiled. "But the good news is, I've regained my stony stare."

"Uh-huh. Right," scoffed the pirate king. Clearly he didn't believe her. Not put off by her snakes in the least, he waved a hand toward them. "I don't know how you managed *this*, but if it means you can't make gold for me any longer, then you aren't worth keeping around, are you? So either make some gold right now to prove you still can, or"—he waved a hand toward Dionysus—"I'll make your friend walk the plank." He grinned evilly. "Speaking of sto-ho-hones, I bet he would sink just like one."

"I'm not joking about my stone gaze," Medusa warned.

"And I'm not joking about the go-ho-hold." Scowling at her, he slammed one fist into the palm of his other hand. "Make some. Now!" When she didn't, the pirate king made good on his threat. He called over two burly pirates—the same ones who had captured and bound her—to get Dionysus.

"No! Stop!" Medusa cried out in alarm. She pointed at the lone stone-dead fish among the fresh ones piled up on the deck just a few feet away. "Look over there if you don't believe me!" she exclaimed.

"What I did to that fish, I can do to you, too. To all of you!" she emphasized, swiveling her head to glare in turn at each member of the crew.

Some of them began to shift their feet and murmur nervously among themselves, but the pirate king only laughed at her. "Ho-ho," he said. "Nice try!"

"I'd listen to her if I were you," Dionysus warned as the burly pirates used their knives to cut through the ropes binding his hands. They hoisted him up like a sack of potatoes and brought him over to where the pirate king stood.

Terrified for her crush, Medusa still held her head high. "Free us at once!" she commanded the pirate king. "Or I'll remove my protective glasses. And then it won't be just your heart that's made of stone!"

To show that that this was no idle threat, Flicka

and Slinky tugged on Medusa's glasses to lift them off her nose a little.

"It's true!" one of the pirates yelled. He'd just come running up from belowdeck, waving a scroll in his hand. "I knew I remembered reading about someone who has a stone gaze and attends that swanky Mount Olympus Academy. I just found the article in an old issue of the *Fierce Pirates Periodical!*" He unfurled the scroll and flashed a drawing of Medusa for everyone to see. "She does have a stone gaze, just like she says!"

With that, he seemed to realize he could be in danger of being turned to stone himself. "Eek!" He turned around and ran belowdecks again, slamming the door behind him. On the way, he tripped, dropping something near Dionysus's feet. A knife!

Panicking now, most of the pirates ran to the

gangplank at the side of the ship and threw themselves overboard to swim to the nearest island. The few who were left—probably the ones who couldn't swim—scrambled up the masts to hide in the crow's nest or among the sails.

"Come back here, you cowards!" the pirate king yelled after them. But they'd heard what the crewman with the scrollazine had said and had seen what Medusa had done to the fish. And they were taking no chances with her and her snakes!

While the pirates were busy jumping ship, Dionysus grabbed the dropped knife. He ran over to Medusa and cut her free.

"Quick! Slice through the grapevines!" she told Dionysus. "Taking them down will signal Aphrodite, Athena, and Artemis that we're ready to catch a ride back to MOA."

As they were tugging the last of the vines off, Aphrodite's swan cart landed in the middle of the deck. No Zeus, Medusa noticed. She wasn't all that surprised he hadn't been found. An hour wasn't a lot of time, and Athena didn't even know exactly where her dad had gone.

Awestruck by the appearance of the magical cart and the beautiful goddessgirls inside it, the pirate king stopped chasing his crew. In fact, as Medusa and Dionysus climbed inside the cart, the few pirates aboard stood rooted to the deck—or clinging to the masts—staring as if they really had become stone statues for a moment.

"Wait," said Medusa, halting her friends' departure. "Should we take that?" She pointed to a chest overflowing with treasure.

Artemis nodded. "I vote yes. Those pirates looted

it from temples and other ships, so we should return it to its rightful owners."

"Yeah!" chorused the others. Quickly Athena cast a spell over the treasure chest to magically lighten it and lift it off the deck into the front of the cart. The three goddessgirls squished together in the front of the cart, leaving the backseat for Medusa and Dionysus. Because the chest took up so much space, Medusa had to sit shoulder to shoulder with Dionysus. Not that she minded!

"No-ho-ho!" wailed the pirate king as he watched the chest being spirited away.

"Ye-hess-hess!" Medusa shouted in return. "Maybe that'll teach you that nothing good comes from stealing!"

As they flew over the Aegean Sea, Medusa and Dionysus filled the others in on their harrowing adventure. They were about halfway back to MOA when they met Zeus and Hera. Zeus was riding Pegasus, while Hera rode right alongside him in her elegant one-seater chariot pulled by peacocks. It turned out that the temple ceremony they'd attended had been in Cyrene, which was on the north African coast, way south of where the goddessgirls had flown.

Zeus's brilliant blue eyes went wide when he suddenly noticed the chest full of treasure, most of it stolen from temples dedicated to him. "Explain!" he commanded.

After Medusa and the others told him what had happened in his absence, he scolded them for going off on such a dangerous journey without him, despite the girls' insistence that they had tried to find him. But then he caught site of the chest again, and boomed, "Well, in the end you did a good job!"

At Hera's suggestion they all landed briefly on an uninhabited island that was no bigger than MOA's gymnasium, and transferred the treasure chest to her chariot. "We'll return all this booty to the temples and ships from which it was stolen," she promised the girls. "Some of it will also come in handy for repairs to the towns and villages damaged during Typhon's rampage."

"Just what I was thinking!" Zeus proclaimed.

Athena winked at Hera. "Yeah, good idea, Dad." It was no secret that Principal Zeus loved to get credit for brilliant ideas and schemes. And he often did come up with them. No matter who'd thought of the idea, it had reminded Medusa about the damage to King Midas's palace and the homes and farms in Phrygia.

As she and her friends were climbing back into

Aphrodite's swan cart to continue on to Mount Olympus, Hera caught Medusa's eye and smiled at her. Then she turned toward Zeus and whispered something into his ear. Principal Zeus nodded, grinning mightily. "You are absolutely right, sugar pie. It was a very daring rescue, and she does deserve a reward."

Reward? Medusa's breath quickened as he swung his gaze toward her. "Just a sec," he told her. He then plunged both of his meaty hands into the treasure chest and rooted around until he came up with a gold necklace that was practically dripping with dazzling green emeralds. It had to be worth a fortune!

"A token of gratitude for your heroism," he said, handing it to Medusa. "Well done."

"Thank you!" Medusa beamed as she took the necklace from him. It was heavier than she'd expected, and she almost dropped it. Truthfully, she wasn't quite sure where she could ever wear such a heavy and luxurious piece of jewelry. And she wondered a little guiltily if she were really deserving of such a reward. She hadn't told Zeus and Hera about the whole golden-touch disaster. But then, no one else had mentioned it either, so she kept mum.

Which reminded her . . . when no one was looking, she whipped off her gold glove and poked one of the emeralds in the necklace with her right index finger. Nothing happened. Ye gods! She really was well and truly free of the golden touch! For real and for sure.

Honk! Honk! Aphrodite's swans had begun to flap their wings. Soon the swan cart was airborne toward Mount Olympus once more. Medusa was already wearing her QoM necklace, so she tucked Zeus's gift necklace into the pocket of her chiton. Unfortunately, with the treasure chest gone, there was now plenty of space in the backseat, so she had no excuse to sit near Dionysus.

Aphrodite, who was the goddessgirl of love after all, must have sensed her disappointment. With an over-the-shoulder grin at Medusa, she directed her swans into an unnecessarily abrupt turn so that the swan cart dipped sideways.

"Whoa!" said Dionysus and the other girls, trying to right themselves.

Meanwhile Medusa slid across the seat and almost landed in Dionysus's lap! "Oops, sorry," she said, pushing back from him some. "Didn't mean to squash you like a pancake."

Dionysus laughed, showing those dimples she always loved. Then he reached for her hand. As the fingers of her right hand twined in his left, she was glad once more to be rid of the golden curse.

"Thanks for the rescue, greenie-girl," Dionysus said softly.

"No problemo-ho," she replied, which made them both laugh.

At that moment Athena turned around to speak to Medusa, but then she burst into giggles, seeming to forget whatever it was she'd been planning to say. Artemis and Aphrodite glanced back and then burst into giggles too.

"What?" asked Medusa.

Dionysus was also grinning at her now. Or more precisely, at the top of her head.

"Are my snakes up to something?" she asked, suddenly suspicious.

Aphrodite pulled a small hand mirror from her pocket and handed it back to Medusa. The cart wobbled momentarily as her mind wandered from her driving. "See for yourself."

With her stoneglasses firmly in place, Medusa angled the mirror so she could better see the top of her head. She blushed when she saw what her snakes had done. They'd looped together in pairs to form six interlocking hearts above her head!

"Ha-ha," she told them. "Very funny, guys." But she said it in a fond tone of voice. She was so happy that her snakes were wiggly and well again that she could put up with a few high jinks. And in all honesty they'd only expressed the liking she truly felt for Dionysus.

"Can I see the necklace Dad gave you?" Athena asked a few moments later.

"Sure," said Medusa. She drew it from her pocket and passed it over the seat to Athena. "It's pretty amazing, but I'm not sure I'll ever actually wear it. I'd be afraid of losing it. And it seems a bit . . ."

"Much?" Artemis supplied, grinning at her over one shoulder.

"Yeah, I was going to say 'grandiose.'"

"You could always sell it," Athena told her, passing it to the other girls to examine as well. "Dad won't mind."

"Mr. Dolos will probably only give me a fraction of its true value," Medusa mused. Still, she could probably buy a *thousand* new chitons with the money she'd make in trade. Only, how many new chitons did she need? she thought as Athena, Aphrodite, and Artemis continued to ooh and aah over the fabulous necklace. She already had five new outfits. That might not seem like very many to someone like Aphrodite, who changed her clothes several times a day, but to her it was plenty.

Her snakes dropped down to nestle lovingly around the base of her neck, and she reached to stroke them with her free hand. Slinky and Pretzel wound around her wrist briefly, then unwound again. It was their version of a hug.

Really, she decided happily, she already had everything she could possibly want now that her snakes had come back to life. And now that Dionysus was safe and sound.

When the others had all admired the necklace, Artemis passed it back to her. Surely she could find a truly good use for the necklace, Medusa thought as she gazed upon it. And in a flash she knew what that use would be.

"Could you drop me off at the IM?" Medusa asked Aphrodite as the swan cart flew over the marketplace. "I've got something I want to do there." In addition to her plans for the necklace, she needed to find suite 142 so she could sign a contract to allow Big D Publications to publish her comics. With all of today's other excitements, she couldn't believe she'd almost forgotten about her Comicontest win!

"I'll go with you," Dionysus said quickly. He hadn't said anything in a while, and she had a feeling there was something on his mind. "We can grab some shakes at the Hungry, Hungry Harpy Café and then borrow pairs of winged sandals at the rental place afterward to get back to MOA."

"Mega-cool," said Medusa. It was sweet of him to offer to go with her. Without him it would be a long walk back to MOA, since she couldn't make winged sandals fly on her own. Or she would have had to wait around to try to hitch a ride back to MOA in Hermes' Delivery Service chariot.

As they landed at the IM, Medusa and Dionysus jumped down from the swan cart. "Later!" Medusa called to her friends. The girls waved good-bye as the cart lifted off again, heading for the Academy.

"First things first," Medusa said as she and Dionysus entered the marketplace. She held up the necklace. "I'm going to put this to good use."

Dionysus cocked an eyebrow, his violet eyes sparkling. "Oh? Can't wait to hear how."

Medusa just smiled at him as she headed for the Hermes' Delivery Service kiosk across from the Green Scene. If Dionysus was surprised when she stopped at the kiosk, he didn't show it. He still seemed preoccupied with something.

He shifted from one foot to the other as she chose a large padded envelope from a pile on the kiosk's counter. While she was paying for the envelope with her last remaining drachma, Dionysus cleared his throat. Finally he said, "I . . . um . . . There's something I've been wanting to ask you . . ."

"Yeah? And what's that?" she asked distractedly as she shoved the necklace into the envelope and then sealed it up. After flipping the envelope over, she grabbed a feather pen from a jar on the counter and began to write.

But instead of continuing with whatever he'd been about to ask, Dionysus's attention switched to the envelope she was writing on. "What are you doing?" he asked curiously.

"What I told you," Medusa said, "putting this

necklace to good use." She showed him the address she'd written on the envelope.

To: King Midas of Phrygia

From: Medusa

For: Disaster Relief

For a second Dionysus just stared at her. Then suddenly he leaned a little closer and kissed her lightly on the cheek before drawing back again. "Greenie-girl, I'm proud of you!"

At his praise, a flood of warm feelings washed over Medusa. A moment like this one was worth more than *any* amount of gold, she thought, still feeling his kiss on her cheek. It was priceless!

He knew how she never had any money. And how she hated having to rely on her sisters for things because of her lack of funds. So he probably figured this was a huge sacrifice. And it sort of was. Still . . .

"I've decided that money isn't everything," she told him, only just then realizing it was true. "However, there are times when it *can* do a lot of good."

With that, she dropped the envelope with the necklace through a slot in the drop-off bin. The packages inside would be loaded onto one of Hermes' delivery chariots later that afternoon.

She turned to Dionysus. "Now we need to find suite 142."

He looked over at the Green Scene across the way. "That's number 114," he said.

"Oh yeah. So it is." Funny how she'd never noticed the numbers beneath the store signs before. Seeing the number 117 on the Mighty Fighty store up ahead, they began to walk in that direction. Along the way

Medusa explained about the comic contest she'd entered and won and how her comics would now be published.

"Comics? Really? That's amazing! Me and the guys love comics," Dionysus said in admiration. "I can't believe you kept this talent of yours hidden all this time. I can't wait to see them. In fact, I want to buy the first copy!"

Medusa blushed, not wanting to admit that she'd been worried about showing her comics to *anyone*. She hadn't been sure they were really any good. "Well, now you know," she said at last.

The numbers on the store signs had been increasing steadily. When they passed the blue door of Ship Shape, the pet supply store, Medusa saw that they were already up to number 140. Then came 141, the Hungry, Hungry Harpy Café. And just past that was . . . Mr. Dolos's Be a Hero store!

Huh? Medusa did a double take, rechecking the number on the sign to make sure she hadn't made a mistake. But underneath the name of the Be a Hero store in small letters and numbers were the words "suite 142." Then it came to her. The *D* in "Big D Publications" must stand for "Dolos"!

The minute they entered the store, the short round shopkeeper—and publisher, too, apparently—took one look at Dionysus and paled. He ran a nervous hand through his slick, black hair, then dropped down behind the counter as if hoping they hadn't seen him.

Dionysus went and leaned over the counter to stare down at him. "Relax," he said. When Dionysus didn't immediately get angry, Mr. Dolos did just that and stood again, smiling sheepishly.

"Ah! And here is the clever creator of the *Queen of Mean!*" he gushed as Medusa came up to the counter too. "Congratulations on winning the very first Big D Publications Comicontest!"

Medusa beamed at him. "Thanks! I'm so happy I won!" Out of the corner of her eye, she saw Dionysus's eyebrows rise at the mention of the Queen of Mean. But she didn't take time to explain. He'd understand the title of her collection as soon as he read one of her comics.

"I have your entry right here," Mr. Dolos said. Turning from the counter, he plucked a bright yellow-and-black-checkered drawstring bag, made from fabric that matched his tunic, from a shelf behind him. He emptied the bag onto the counter.

All ten of Medusa's comic scrolls rolled out.

"May I?" asked Dionysus, picking up one of them.

When Medusa nodded, he eagerly unrolled it and began to read. She held her breath, hoping he'd like it.

"I can hardly wait to display these in the store's window," Mr. Dolos said, drawing her attention. "I am absitively posolutely certain that customers will find them very entertaining!" After digging around under the counter, he produced a printed sheet of papyrus. "But first I'll need you to sign this permissions letter."

Just then Dionysus laughed out loud. "Ha!" he said. "A magic cheese! I love it!"

Smiling at his response, Medusa read through the permissions letter carefully. It was easy to do, since the letter was short:

240

I, THE UNDERSIGNED, GRANT BIG D
PUBLICATIONS THE RIGHT TO DISPLAY MY
COMIC-SCROLL COLLECTION FOR A LIMITED
TIME IN THE WINDOW OF THE IMMORTAL
MARKETPLACE'S BE A HERO STORE.

There was a space for her signature at the bottom of the letter. Confused, she flipped the letter over, but the other side was blank. "Where's the part about publication?" she asked. "Is there a page missing?"

"Publication?" echoed Mr. Dolos. "No, nothing's missing." He handed her a feather quill pen. "Perhaps you misunderstood. The grand prize is having your comics displayed in my store's window. Just think of all the people who will see them!"

Medusa's heart sank. "But you used the name Big D *Publications*," she pointed out. "You offered a *contract.* So I thought the prize would be a publishing contract, not just display rights." Her snakes, who'd been dozing peacefully at the back of her neck, awoke abruptly. Sensing her disappointment, and that Mr. Dolos was the source of it, they darted their heads toward him, flicking their tongues and hissing.

Hearing them, Dionysus looked up from the comic-scroll he'd been reading. He frowned at Mr. Dolos, who gulped. "Is there a problem?" Dionysus asked.

A fine sheen of sweat broke out on Mr. Dolos's forehead. He whipped out a black-and-yellow-checkered handkerchief and mopped at his forehead. "Um . . . not at all." Keeping a wary eye on Dionysus and on Medusa's snakes, too, he asked, "Just how many copies of your collection were you expecting my company to publish?"

Medusa toyed with the QoM charm on her necklace, considering the matter. She'd want copies for herself, for Dionysus, and for some of her friends, of course. And maybe even for her sisters and her parents. She counted in her head. "Twenty copies should do it," she concluded.

Mr. Dolos breathed a sigh of apparent relief. "Deal!" he said. "You can pick them up here in the store one week from today."

Relieved as well, Medusa scribbled her signature on the permissions letter. When she handed it over to Mr. Dolos, he studied her hands. "No glove, I see," he commented. "I hope that doesn't mean you won't be wanting to exchange more gold objects?"

She'd never told Mr. Dolos that she had the golden touch, but he must have figured it out. Either that or her sisters had shared their suspicions when they'd gone to talk to him behind her back. "No more gold. Sorry," she said with a quick glance at Dionysus. She hadn't told him about the purchases she'd made when she'd first gotten the golden touch, but since he was still absorbed in her comic-scroll and didn't seem to hear, she decided there really wasn't any need to.

The two of them left the store shortly thereafter. After stopping for shakes at the café, they held hands and chatted about general stuff while skimming back to the Academy in rented winged sandals. They were almost over the MOA courtyard when Medusa said, "I just remembered there was something you wanted to ask me when I was mailing that necklace to King Midas. What was it?"

For some reason Dionysus looked startled. His

arm jerked a little, and she felt her hand slip from his. She grabbed at him and missed. "No! I'm falling!" she yelped. This was one of her worst nightmares. But before she could tumble to the marble tiles below, Dionysus swooped down and caught her in his arms.

"Got you!" he said. Then he gently set her down on a bench at the edge of the courtyard. He took a deep breath, then said, "I'm sorry!"

"It's okay," she replied a little shakily.

He ran his fingers through his curly hair. "I wasn't . . . I mean, I was just kind of nervous about what I wanted to ask you before . . . because I know you think the whole idea is kind of dumb, but . . . the Temple Games are in two weeks, and . . ." Looking flustered, he ground to a halt.

Medusa adored the fact that this cute, violet-eyed godboy, star of almost all the school plays, could still become tongue-tied at times. She decided to put him out of his misery. "The answer is *yes*," she said with a grin. "I'd love to champion you at the games and cheer you on big-time!"

"You would?" Dionysus asked, like he couldn't quite believe he'd heard her correctly. When she nodded, he jumped up and pumped a fist in the air. "Woo-hoo!"

"One thing, though," she said, standing up too. "I'm a pretty awesome swimmer, so I'm thinking I'll join the games myself. So maybe we could be on the same team and you could be my champion as well?" She touched the QoM charm on her necklace at her throat. "In fact, this'll be my favor. You could wear it in the games for luck. You know, like when Hera gave Zeus her lace handkerchief."

He looked startled for a moment, but then as his gaze fell on the necklace she always wore, a realization dawned. "Hey! QoM. I just got what that necklace charm of yours stands for. The *Queen of Mean*. Your comics, right?"

She laughed, nodding.

"Sure I'll wear it. I'll give you a favor too, and we'll be each other's champions!"

It wasn't every guy who'd wear his crush's necklace. Her crush was so awesome! Without thinking, she lifted on tiptoe and planted a light kiss on his cheek right in front of the other students who happened to be in the courtyard too. She could hardly believe she'd done that. It made two kisses in a single day!

"Woo-hoo!" he whooped again.

As they walked across the courtyard a few minutes

later, Medusa glanced toward the gym. "I wonder if Poseidon has been able to fix the pool." When Dionysus sent her a questioning look, she remembered she'd forgotten to tell him about turning the pool's water to gold.

After she explained, he said, "I've still got a few drops of the magic river water left. It should do the trick if Poseidon was unable to reverse things. You go on ahead, and I'll check."

"Thanks," Medusa said gratefully. "See you later," she called, taking the steps leading up to the Academy's front doors.

She hadn't been back in her room for more than a few minutes when her sisters knocked on her door. "So you're back," Stheno said, flopping down on Medusa's spare bed. "We came by a little while ago. Where were you?"

"Long story," said Medusa. But before she could begin to explain all that had happened, Euryale interrupted.

"Save it for later, Dusa," she said, dropping to lie down on the bed Medusa usually slept in. "We're zonked. We've been gone all day. After Mom and Dad left, we went shopping at a brand-new market-place that just opened up in Thebes."

"Yeah, shopping is so tiring," Stheno put in. Medusa sat on her desk chair, since her sisters were hogging both beds. "They've got an even bigger Green Scene there than the one at the IM."

"And we ran up some pretty big bills," Euryale said, getting to the real reason for their visit. "So we need you to hand over more drachmas or make us some gold. Now would be good."

"Sure," said Medusa. As quick as a wink she jumped

up and went from one bed to the other, touching each of her sisters with her right index finger.

Shrieking, they leaped to their feet. "What did you do that for?" yelled Euryale.

"Now we'll turn into . . ." Stheno's words died away as she looked down at herself and saw she hadn't changed to gold. Her sisters stared at each other, then back at Medusa, not getting it. "Hey, where's your glove?"

Medusa grinned big and waved her ungloved right hand in the air. "My golden curse . . . um . . . *touch* is gone. I've been cured."

"*What?*" both sisters exclaimed in horror.

"But that's terrible!" Stheno said. She looked a bit greener than usual—quite ill, as a matter of fact. "You have to get Dionysus to give you the touch again. Or maybe you could talk him into giving us the golden touch? Or at least telling us the spell so we can give the touch to ourselves?"

Medusa folded her arms over her chest and shook her head. "No way."

"But," said Euryale, her voice sounding anxious, "how will we pay our bills?" She glanced around the room. "You must have *some* gold left."

"So you want to borrow money from *me* now?" Medusa asked, quirking an eyebrow in amusement. Talk about a reversal!

"You could give us that jellyfish pin," Stheno said, her eyes zeroing in on the front of Medusa's chiton.

Medusa's hand went up to feel the pin. She had forgotten she was wearing it. Would she miss it? she wondered. Until the past few days, she'd never worn it much anyway. She just didn't wear that much jewelry. Only her QoM necklace most of the time. "All right," she said at last.

As she began to unfasten the pin, Stheno's eyes widened in surprise. "Really?" she said to Medusa. "That's very decent of—"

"So what's the catch?" Euryale interrupted to ask. "What's it going to cost us?"

Cost them? Medusa hadn't thought about asking for anything in return. "How about a dozen room cleanings?" she joked. "Apiece."

Her sisters blanched.

"Just kidding," Medusa told them quickly. She wouldn't want her sisters messing around in her room anyway. She liked keeping her stuff private. And frankly she was tired of her interactions with her sisters always involving exchanges of favors.

"Tell you what," she said to them as she held the

jellyfish pin out to Stheno. "You can have this for free. All I ask for in return is your undying gratitude."

"Huh?" said Euryale. "What's that supposed to mean?"

But Stheno seemed to understand. She smiled at Medusa as she took the pin. "Thanks, Dusa. I really, um, appreciate this. And we are . . . grateful, right, Euryale?"

Euryale looked at Stheno like she was nutso, but then rolled her eyes. "Yeah, I guess it was actually pretty nice of you, Dusa," she said on her way out the door.

As Medusa closed her door behind her sisters, she realized she'd forgotten to tell them about her comic-scroll contest win. She started to call them back, then stopped herself. Although she planned to give them copies, they weren't likely to enjoy how she'd depicted them. In fact, those comics would probably put Stheno's undying gratitude to the test. On the other hand, even Euryale might be nicer to her in the future if she became worried that Medusa might write more comics that revealed the unflattering truth of how her sisters treated her!

She grinned at the thought. Then her stomach growled, and she remembered that the shake with Dionysus in the IM café had been the sum total of lunch. She'd had nothing else to eat since breakfast. Neither had her snakes.

"Sorry, guys. Who's hungry?" Her snakes stood up straight on her head as if all raising their hands to say, *I am!*

She opened her closet and took out a snake snack sack. Then she tossed a handful of dried peas and carrot curls into the air. *Snap! Snap!*

"I struck gold the day I got you guys," she told them, smiling softly as joy filled her. "And I never, never, never, never, never, never, never, never, never, never, never, never want to lose you again. That's twelve 'never's, one for each of you."

They wiggled their heads up and down, nodding to show her the feeling was mutual. Then, as she tossed up more peas and carrots, they gobbled down the snacks.

Snap! Snap! Snap! Snap! Snap! Snap! Snap! Snap! Snap! Snap! Snap! Snap!